scandalized

BACKSTAGE PASS #1

TARA FREJAS

*Scandal*ized

This book is a work of fiction.

While inspired by real people and events,
all characters, events, and some places depicted
in this book are entirely fictional.

This book or any portion thereof may not be reproduced or
used in any manner whatsoever without the express written
permission of the publisher except for the use of brief
quotations in a book review.

Cover illustration | Shaira Bea San Jose
Calligraphy | Porcupine Strongwill
Design & Layout | Tara Frejas

Edited by Layla Tanjutco

To you with the heart of a K-Pop fan,
and *you*, for whom that heart goes *dugeun-dugeun*.

A NOTE FROM THE AUTHOR

When I first wrote the draft for *Scandalized* in 2015—for #SparkNA, the very first Mina V. Esguerra facilitated workshop I joined—I'd already envisioned myself creating a series in this universe. I had initially called the series *Roadie Romance* in honor of the first book's main character, but belatedly realized she wasn't the *only* main character I was going to highlight in the future books.

Hence, a series name change: *Backstage Pass.*

This re-released version of *Scandalized*, though still essentially the same story you might have already read, is an improved edition. Minor changes in tense and point-of-view have been done for a better reading experience.

Included in this version are two bonus short stories, previously published elsewhere. *Gabriel's Checklist* was part of the #romanceclass Christmas anthology *Make My Wish Come True* (2016), and *548* was a contribution to *#SayFeels* (2017), a Valentine's special by The Reading Belles. In this edition, you will also find the full versions of East Genesis Project's songs *Golden* and *Without Fail.*

Thank you, and I hope you enjoy reading or rereading…enough to want the second book in the series, coming very soon.

TRACK ONE

ZERO/HERO

"I GUESS IT'S A SLOW NEWS DAY, HUH?"

Three heads bent over an iPad simultaneously looked up at the sound of Jo Yihwan's voice.

"Have you seen these comments?" Steven Bae, the currently ash blond drummer of East Genesis Project, asked. He slid the gadget across the glass table toward Yihwan, who only gave the screen a passing glance. The band leader let out a soft, dismissive laugh seeing a glamour photo of himself posted beside a grainy screenshot of a video taken at the film premiere they attended last night.

Jo Yihwan, Knight in Shining Armor, the headline read.

The rest of the article lauded him as a hero for helping prevent a stampede from breaking out at the event. It already had more than a thousand comments and several hundred shares, making Yihwan's name trend across all South Korean search engines.

"Stop wasting your time on the internet, Steven," Yihwan said with a sigh, shaking his head. He nudged the gadget back to his bandmate, spared a glance at the two other people sitting on either side of Steven—bassist/vocalist Song Minchan, and Fi Legaspi, their road manager—and added, "People just like exaggerating stuff online."

"Um, these *people* you speak of? They *buy* our albums," Steven pointed out as Yihwan padded to the music space in their dorm. "I'm willing to bet we'll be able to sell several hundred units of *Genesis* and *Sophomore Year* by the end of the week."

"Yeah. Remember the time Minchan went on *Running Man*—" Fi blurted out, pausing when the person in question scowled at her.

"Noona…" Minchan murmured the syllables as though Fi did him a grave injustice. The pout on his lips drew out a chuckle from her.

She flashed him a peace sign. "Mianhae, Chan-ah."

1

Too late. Yihwan and Steven were already having a giggle fit, possibly recalling their magnae's accidental follies on the show.

Although the youngest EG Project member vowed never to go on any variety show again, he couldn't deny his one-time appearance on the game show was a blessing in disguise. A lot of the show's female viewers found Minchan so adorable they decided to give the band's music a try as soon as the broadcast ended. In less than a week, their debut album, *Genesis*—already three-and-a-half years old then—suddenly rose on the charts.

Steven's prediction might not be far off the mark.

"What I'm saying is, this could be a good thing for us." Steven handed his iPad over to Fi and winked at her. "Right, Fi?"

"Of course."

Minchan agreed. "It's good not to be forgotten, especially since we've spent most of last year in Japan."

Steven snapped his fingers and got up from the couch, following Yihwan into the music space. "We're all set then. Our next album's going to be a huge hit, thanks to our dear leader-nim."

"Our next album hasn't even been written yet." Yihwan ran a hand through his messy tuft of dark brown hair and pulled his favorite black Stratocaster off the guitar rack. Steven, meanwhile, sat on his self-proclaimed throne behind his LED-lit Pearl drum set.

"We're really just subtly nagging you to hurry up with the songwriting, hyung." Minchan said, before nicking a slice of kimbap from the platter on the glass table and joining his hyung-deul for a quick rehearsal.

"Hey!" Yihwan protested. "We agreed to write ten songs each!"

Steven twirled a drumstick between his fingers. "I'm already on song number 7."

"Song number 4!" Minchan piped in before popping the kimbap into his mouth.

Yihwan blinked. It had only been two weeks since they'd agreed on a ten-song assignment for a new album. How was it possible for Steven and Minchan (who whined so much about it too) to have made this much progress?

More importantly, why was his slate still blank?

Everyone called Jo Yihwan a natural in songwriting and composition. In fact, he wrote and composed 90% of EG Project's discography. The abundant praise he got for his work never really bothered him until the more recent articles about the band made it sound as though he was the only person in the group who mattered. Journalists who sought them out for interviews rarely had any questions for Steven and Minchan, and the write-ups have started to bear his name instead of the band's.

He found that unfair. His band members deserved to be recognized for their hard work too.

Hence, the ten-song assignment. Yihwan challenged his band members to write and compose ten songs each, after which they would determine which songs they want to include in their new album.

He felt inadequate now, having been unable to write a single verse since the challenge commenced. Inspiration seemed to have eluded him lately, and he kept convincing himself it was only because he didn't have the luxury to just *sit down and write*.

But it wasn't like Steven and Minchan were complaining. There was hardly any reason to, especially since their successful seven-city Japanese album tour had just ended. They did miss performing for their fans in South Korea, but these first few weeks of freedom allowed them to breathe a little and catch up on sleep, among other things. For the first time in almost a year, their daily schedules didn't involve being up and about for more than twenty hours a day.

"Relax. We're not really in a hurry, are we?" Fi asked, snapping Yihwan out of his trance.

"No," they replied in unison.

The roadie smiled. "Then you shouldn't be worried. The reason why Amethyst Entertainment isn't pressuring you to come up with something new just yet is because they're still basking in the afterglow of all the money you brought in...*and* the money you will continue to cash in when the Asian tour begins."

"Ahh, I wish I could bask in *that* afterglow, too," said Steven.

3

Minchan shook his head. "You would, if you'd stop dating all those women."

Fi snapped her fingers. "Focus, please. I want this rehearsal done in two hours," she demanded with a tap-tap-tap on her wristwatch before Steven could blurt out something in protest. She pulled out a couple thousand won from her pocket and placed it on the table like a bar customer ordering a round of shots. "I'm buying chimaek for dinner."

Steven pointed a drum stick at Fi. "Ooh, I like this one!"

Yihwan just laughed, pulled the mic stand in front of him and spoke into the unplugged microphone. "Any requests, pretty lady?"

"*Stuff of Daydreams*, please."

And without further ado, Steven hit his drumsticks. *1, 2, 3, 4...*

Three days later

In the quiet of a small meeting room, Fi plugged a pair of earphones into her ears and organized her band's schedules for the week. She tapped her feet and hummed quietly to the music, pausing when the opening riff to EG Project's first single came on.

> *So it's like this, let me tell you how it is*
> *I would hold you in my arms*
> *say 'I love you' with a kiss, kiss, kiss*
> *Our every single day would be*
> *the very best, no less—but I guess*
> *nothing is ever as it seems*
> *every single thing is the stuff of daydreams*

None of all the other EG Project songs have resonated as strongly with Fi as Stuff of Daydreams had. In fact, she found herself wondering time and again if Jo Yihwan had somehow taken a peek inside her heart and decided to write about the secrets it once held.

That wasn't possible, of course.

How could he, when he was so busy looking at someone else?

"Noona...."

A gentle hand rested on her shoulder, disrupting her thoughts. She looked up, mildly surprised to see Minchan. When had he entered the room?

"Noona, look at this," he said, placing an iPad on the table.

She mumbled an "oh no" as soon as her gaze fell on the screen, on a photo of Yihwan and top actress Han Haera posted side by side. Above them were the words: *Are EG Project's Jo Yihwan and National Goddess Han Haera Dating?*

"No, no, no..." Fi brusquely pulled her earphones off and looked at Minchan. "Where's Yihwan?"

"I saw him with Minja noona a couple of hours ago. I think they were discussing the upcoming tour."

Fi stood up, spaced out for a few seconds, and sat back down again.

How can this be happening?

Yihwan and Haera were a closely guarded secret, a hush-hush relationship only a handful of trusted people know. But while the couple had broken up a long time ago, news like this wouldn't die unless either of the parties released a statement.

She got up again, gathered her things.

"Where are you going, noona?"

"To find Yihwan. Or Gabriel. Whoever crosses my path first."

News got to Yihwan before Fi could.

When she found him alone inside the Opal rehearsal studio, Fi confirmed his distress at his unfocused gaze and how he unnecessarily shifted his weight in front of the piano.

They didn't breathe a word to each other for a long while.

The silence was broken when the door behind her opened, letting Steven and Minchan in. When Yihwan turned to look at them, Fi could swear she saw the two members flinch from the corner of her eye.

"Come on, you guys." A tone of practiced nonchalance came out of Yihwan. "Give it a few days and everyone will be talking about something else."

"Are you all right, hyung?" Minchan asked. He was a step behind Steven, and though he stood taller than both his hyung-deul, to Fi he appeared like a child cowering behind his older brother.

"Sure."

Yihwan's fingers hit the keys, filling the room with a melancholy melody Fi hadn't heard before. Right away, she recognized its potential and wondered if he was working on his ten-song challenge. "Has any news about Steven dating anyone lasted over a week?" he added.

That was their cue to laugh, but no one dared.

Because it wasn't funny sitting in the front row, watching Haera break Yihwan's heart. It wasn't funny how, even if the breakup was almost two years ago, the band leader had never really moved on. Haera had since become an invisible imprint on all of his songs—a phrase here, a refrain there—and Fi wondered how Yihwan would deal with netizen backlash once this skeleton gets dragged out of its closet.

And how *she* would.

[BREAKING] Are EG Project's Jo Yihwan and National Goddess Han Haera Dating?

June 30 | Scoop News

Speculations about a dating scandal between Jo Yihwan and actress Han Haera have surfaced.

A very reliable source revealed that the couple began dating in 2012, a year after Jo's band, East Genesis Project, debuted. That same year, Han moved to Choigo Entertainment after her contract with Amethyst Entertainment ended. She went on to star in a string of blockbuster hits, starting with *She Who Must Not Be Loved*.

The source says, "It's a very low-key, very intimate relationship. They usually enjoy car dates and very rarely go out in public. I believe they are still together."

Last year, Choigo Entertainment confirmed that Han and co-actor Jung Hwichan begun dating after filming their hit movie *Six Ways to Sunday*. The lovebirds have since been spotted going on several dates around Seoul and, very recently, overseas.

Both Amethyst Entertainment and Choigo Entertainment have yet to release official statements about this issue.

COMMENTS

[+8,675, -987] This is such a joke. Han Haera looks good and all, but she's a bitch. Yihwannie matches well with someone else. Like Steven Bae. ㅋㅋㅋ

[+6,119, -1,024] Is Han Haera cheating on these two fine men? Heol. Guess being born with that face gives you license to play around.

[+4,634, -1,055] Jo Yihwan seems like a good boy and all, but they're not on the same level. Han Haera is better off with Jung Hwichan.

[+2,978, -500] What if it was Jung Hwichan who stole Han Haera away from Jo Yihwan? Daebak. A real life makjang drama.

[+1,450, -598] YIHWAN OPPA, NO! I heard that Han Haera is a diva in real life. You don't deserve someone like her. Please never date.

TRACK TWO
그냥 해라 /JUST HAERA

AT 9:15 A.M., GABRIEL PARK made a beeline from his desk to the vending machine down the hall. Fifteen minutes into this work day and he was already feeling the need for a second dose of caffeine. Maybe even a third, because god knows how small these vending machine cups were.

As the machine slowly dispensed his choice of poison, the 27-year old public relations manager sighed at the prospect of being stuck behind his desk all day and coming up with various versions of "No comment."

Amazing, he thought. Not even 24 hours had passed since the first Jo Yihwan-Han Haera article was released on the internet, yet it had already been taken apart, spun around, and turned inside out at lightning speed. A single story progressed from a seed to a full-grown tree, now adorned with so-called sources and questionable, badly-taken photos.

"Amethyst..." He managed a decent tone when he answered the phone on his desk. He hadn't even taken a sip of his coffee yet.

"This is Kim Yeonmi of *Showbiz Seoul*. May I please get a statement about the rumors concerning Jo Yihw—"

He kept his answer curt—"I'm sorry, we don't have a statement for this yet"—and put the receiver down.

It rang again.

Gabriel looked around and saw all of his teammates on their phones, picking up calls and hanging up after uttering a grand total of ten words. Until Jo Yihwan returns from a shoot in Cheongdam-dong and has a few minutes to sit down with them and clarify things, it was the public relations team's job to hold the fort.

For a brief moment, Gabriel considered divulging everything he knew about Yihwan and Haera to the next person who called, but it was precisely because he knew so much that he needed to shut up.

"Ameth—"

"Lee Buyoung, *Daily Entertainment*. A comment on..."

"None at the moment, I'm sorry."

He finally took a sip of coffee as his sunbae—Shin Minja, a married woman in her forties—motioned for him to come to the window. Her gentle gesture turned aggressive when he did nothing but sit there and gape at her, clueless. Taking his tiny paper cup with him, Gabriel ignored the ringing phone on his desk and approached the window.

What the fuck.

It wasn't like he'd never seen fans gathered in droves like this, holding signs and pearl gold balloons in support of Amethyst Entertainment's first and most popular artist, but the energy was different today. The crowd was hostile, and they weren't screaming "Stay healthy!" or "Good job!" or "We love you!"

Instead, they were yelling for Jo Yihwan to tell them the truth, as though the band leader had an obligation to tell them *everything.*

South Korean entertainment was a curious, curious thing. Gabriel learned this first-hand when he relocated from New York to Seoul over three years ago and took a job at Amethyst Entertainment's PR Department. Although born to Korean parents, he grew up on the side of the world where people didn't care as much when news about their favorite celebrities getting into relationships broke out. Sure, there would be buzz here and there. If you were famous enough, a dedicated bunch of paparazzi waiting outside your house was just about as normal as getting your daily paper. If you were notorious for something, though, that meant more paps at your tail.

But none of that, he imagined, compared to the discomfort and inconvenience sasaeng fans could work themselves up to. They were a different breed. Gabriel still shuddered at the stories he's heard from his colleagues—of fans breaking into artists' homes to steal underwear, sending letters written with their own blood, or trying to poison their idol's rival.

The stories didn't end there.

"Someone get another batch of security people down there," Minja said to no one in particular. She shook her head, looked at her broad-shouldered hoobae, and swiped the cup of coffee he was holding. "God, I hope I never see my daughter in one of these things one day..."

Gabriel chuckled lightly and thought, *There goes my coffee.* Lingering by the window, he stared blankly at the crowd and sighed.

"Well. Good morning to you too, Gabe," he muttered to himself and went back to work.

"That one. And that one," Minchan pointed out, waving his ice cream spoon left and right as soon as the driver pulled up in front of a photo studio in Cheongdam-dong. He seemed to be pointing at a woman pushing a stroller away from them, and a man leaning against a lamppost outside a boutique.

Steven turned to Minchan, frowning. "Are you high? Those people can't be paparazzi."

"You're just slow."

As soon as the van door slid open, Fi hopped out to fetch Yihwan from his photo shoot. She pointed at both Steven and Minchan. "I want this bickering done before we get back."

"Can I slap him a little?" Minchan's eyes turned into uneven crescents when he laughed.

Fi only chuckled and shut the door, rushing to the studio lobby afterward. She made a dash for the second floor as soon as the receptionist informed her of Yihwan's whereabouts. But before she could knock on his dressing room door, Fi heard Yihwan's voice.

"Was that an accusation? Are you even listening to yourself?"

She froze. *Is he talking to—*

"Haera. Noona, could you lis...hello? Hello?" A dull slam followed, and then, silence. Fi's heart sank to her stomach.

She pressed her ear against the door and heard a bit of shuffling inside, heavy and hurried, as though Yihwan was shoving things into his bag with the force of a punch. Taking a deep breath, Fi knocked lightly, the rhythm mimicking the steady opening beat of *Stuff of Daydreams*.

The door swung open, revealing Yihwan in a dark blue V-neck and faded jeans. The eyeliner he still had on made his eyes look fiercer than they should be. Either that, or he still had not blinked away his frustration over that phone call.

"Hey, Fi! Are the boys downstairs?" he asked in a tone too cheerful to be genuine.

"Yeah, picked them up from recording." She stepped inside the dressing room and found it difficult to breathe, as if the heated conversation she inadvertently overheard had sucked the air out of the small space. Fi managed a smile anyway, even if seeing Yihwan put on an act weighed her heart down. "We should hurry back before Steven dies at Minchan's hands."

That made the band leader smile. It was small but sincere, more than Fi can ask for.

"What are they arguing about *now*?"

"Paparazzi. Minchan's been pointing them out to Steven, but Steven doesn't believe him."

"I saw two outside," Yihwan said, beating Fi to reaching for his bag. She frowned at him, gestured for him to *give it, now*. He merely shook his head and grinned.

"At the rate you're going, you won't be needing me anymore."

"Come on, Fi. I can't let you carry all my stuff."

Fi was reminded once again how Yihwan's always been big on chivalry, how he was raised to treat people with kindness and respect. That didn't stop her from snatching his bag from him while he was distracted, though, and she sped past him like a petty thief as he said his good-byes and thank yous to the photographer and her crew.

It was too late for him to protest; Fi had already disappeared down the stairwell.

Perhaps it was a good thing that the trip back to AmEnt was filled with lighthearted conversation and laughter, because as soon as they entered the building, things turned tense. They headed straight to one of the conference rooms where Mr. Jin—the interim CEO's executive assistant—was waiting with three managers from the PR department, Gabriel Park included.

After being questioned about his relationship with Haera, Yihwan finally admitted to dating her for a year.

"We broke up while she was shooting her third film. EG Project was also preparing for a comeback then. Things got busy and we naturally drifted apart," he revealed. "It was an amicable breakup."

Both Fi and Gabriel looked up at Yihwan when he said this. So did Steven and Minchan.

Ah, Fi thought. *Jo Yihwan is capable of lying, after all.*

It was Gabriel who came out with the game changer: "Choigo Entertainment wants us to deny it. They've been calling all morning, asking us to align our press releases. They're saying the news is starting to hurt Haera's image."

"Then let's deny it."

Fi's eyes widened. She couldn't believe Yihwan was throwing in the towel just like that.

"It's just Han Haera," he said, shrugging. *Just the woman he loved, no big deal.* "If it makes everyone's job easier, let's deny it."

Text Log: Jo Yihwan & Han Haera
June 30

> Jo Yihwan, 10:54 pm
> You're getting what you want. Like always.

Han Haera, 11:00 pm
I'm so sorry, Yihwan-ah.
You misunderstood what I was trying to say.

> Jo Yihwan, 11:23 pm
> I'm really not in the mood for any more apologies.

Han Haera, 11:35 pm
Yihwan-ah. Don't be like this.
You know what people are going to say
if we don't clear things up right away.

> Jo Yihwan, 11:39 pm
> I know.
> And that's precisely why,
> as of today, we never happened.

Han Haera, 11:50 pm
You know this is not what I wanted.

> Jo Yihwan, 11:54 pm
> Hard to believe when you've accused me of
> using you for my band's tour publicity.

Han Haera, 12:08 am
I wasn't thinking straight when I said that.
I'm so sorry. I know you wouldn't do that to me.

> Jo Yihwan, 12:18 am
> I brought this upon myself. Just be happy.

TRACK THREE
CUTS & BURNS

YIHWAN CALLED IT A DAY at six in the evening, Steven reported.

Anyone who knew the band leader well would say this was uncharacteristic of him, *especially* when they were in the middle of tour preparations. The fact that he asked Steven and Minchan to leave him at the studio so he could do some writing was even more worrisome, at least to Fi.

"Remind me again why he wanted that music space set up at the dorm," she said, eyes scanning Steven and Minchan's faces. Neither of them looked agitated, so she ruled out the possibility of a fight. "Wasn't it so he could have a place to write his songs?"

Both boys shrugged.

"All right. I'll stay behind as well. I'll see you tomorrow."

Both boys nodded and acknowledged Gabriel, with whom Fi was having coffee at the employee lounge, before leaving. She watched them enter the elevator before turning to Gabriel. "I have to go check on Yihwan."

"You might want to leave him alone for now, Fi." He picked up the cup she abandoned beside him and dangled it between his thumb and middle finger, to remind her to return to their disrupted conversation.

A sigh. "Fifteen minutes."

Gabriel smiled when she made her way back to the couch. "Thirty."

"Twenty."

"Relax, Filipina. He's not going to slash his wrists over this," he said, handing the cup of coffee to her. "At least not literally."

Fi took the cup, sat beside him, and frowned. "That doesn't make me feel any better."

Filipina Legaspi used to blame herself for the tragedy that was Jo Yihwan's heartbreak.

Her first assignment as an industry rookie was to manage Han Haera's wardrobe. Although her stint as part of the actress' entourage was short-lived, it had been a good opportunity for her to learn the ropes. She got to know who was who, what went where, and the basic dos and don'ts when working in the entertainment industry.

It was around that time that she had her first encounter with three trainees who would eventually become her band, East Genesis Project.

The boys had been loitering down the hall that led to the rehearsal rooms, and she found out as she passed them that they had been waiting for *her*, the "new girl in Han Haera's entourage." All because Yihwan, the lanky one with unruly red hair and mismatched pair of sneakers, had a favor to ask.

It felt rather juvenile, and Fi couldn't help but chuckle softly when she learned of the request. She liked how straightforward Yihwan was, telling her he needed her help in getting a message through to Han Haera. Apparently, no one else in her old entourage had given the trainee the time of day.

Fi found it cute when a folded note was anxiously entrusted to her.

Han Haera thought the same twenty-four hours later, and the rest, as they say, was history.

"The article isn't getting released to the press till morning. We still have time."

Yihwan didn't look up from his piano playing. Fi suspected he was simmering inside, and the ivories had no choice but to bear the brunt of his frustration. With a sigh, she crossed the room, plopped down on the two-seater couch behind him, and waited.

It seemed that with Yihwan, she was always waiting.

16

And it wasn't his fault, really.

Aside from having excellent social and communication skills, another thing a road manager should be good at is waiting. For callbacks, endorsement offers, TV appearance requests. For costume fittings, rehearsals, recordings, and everything else in between.

The only thing not in the job description was waiting for the band leader to fall in love.

You're like the proverbial moth to the flame, Gabriel told her a while back, as she numbed the pain in her chest with makgeolli. Somehow, the handsome new PR manager transformed into a six-foot-two sounding board where her unrequited love for Yihwan was concerned.

Just my luck that he's a fucking bonfire.

Fi was almost convinced she was hungover when she opened her eyes, disoriented and with a stinging pain in her neck. She turned her head and saw Yihwan sitting beside her, writing something in his notebook. The sudden movement aggravated the pain, making her yelp and grab the side of her neck.

"Oh good. You're awake," he said. "Stiff neck?"

"Yeah. What time is it?"

"Three a.m."

"Whaaat."

Yihwan began tucking things away in a folder, then into a bag. Fi spied Haera's name scribbled on one loose song sheet before it was filed into another folder, out of her sight.

"Why didn't you just wake me up?" The light coming from down the hall made her squint, but Fi noted a hint of a smile on Yihwan's lips. It's the mischievous sort, one that made her suspicious enough to want to check her reflection in the mirror right that moment.

And as though he had read her mind, Yihwan said, "I didn't write anything on your face. You were sleeping so soundly, I just didn't have the heart to wake you."

"Like you didn't have the heart to answer a damn question five hours ago?"

17

The band leader lost what little shade of cheer he had on his face and merely offered his hand to her when he got up. "Let's go home. I'm really tired."

Fi stared at his ink-stained palm and took it, wondering how many of the words he spilled on paper tonight spelled out Haera's name.

[BREAKING NEWS] Amethyst Entertainment: "Jo Yihwan and Han Haera never dated."

July 1 | yesul.co.kr

"Jo Yihwan and Han Haera never dated."

Amethyst Entertainment released this official statement today, dispelling the quickly spreading rumors about East Genesis Project's band leader and the National Goddess.

"It's true that they met while Han Haera was still signed under Amethyst Entertainment, but they only had a senior-junior relationship. Back then, the agency was still small, and it wasn't unusual to see the artists and trainees going out for impromptu gatherings after a hard day's work."

The agency revealed that the band is not taking any legal action against the people who spread the rumors at the moment, as they are focusing their time and effort on their upcoming Asian tour.

"EG Project has always been very thankful for their fans' support and hope that they continue to show their love as they embark on a new journey."

COMMENTS

[+12,690, -2,234] The rumors were baseless to begin with. No names, no evidence. Even those photos weren't convincing enough. Now I wonder if it's Amethyst that did the stirring up, or Choigo. Both EG Project and Han Haera have projects coming up... they needed ALL the publicity!

[+8,104, -456] THANK GOD IT'S NOT TRUE. Even if Han Haera is a top actress, I wouldn't want Jo Yihwan to be involved in this mess.

[+7,005, -898] So when are we hearing a statement from Amethyst about YiVen? ㅋㅋㅋ

[+4,102, -1,987] Steven Bae likes this post.

[+2,125, -2,087] Han Haera and Jung Hwichan forever! <3333 JUST GET MARRIED ALREADY SO THESE RUMORS WOULD STOP CIRCULATING!

FOUR

TAKE A SWIG

"**S**OMETHING'S OFF with Yihwan hyung," Minchan quietly declared to Steven after the leader told them to "take ten."

"Thank God I'm not the only one who noticed. I was beginning to question my sanity when he kept switching arrangements during the *Firefly Dreams* and *Something There* mashup!"

They both glanced at Yihwan, now crouched by the edge of the main stage, speaking to a sound engineer. Tonight was the last night of technical rehearsals at the Jamsil Indoor Stadium that would officially kick off their *Leap of Faith* tour.

It wasn't the best time to doubt your band leader's ability to keep himself together in time for the concert.

"And didn't we change the intro to the *Sophomore Year* medley?" Steven asked, picking up the music sheets lying by his feet to double check. They *had* indeed agreed to change the intro to the medley, something Yihwan seemed to have forgotten during rehearsal, throwing both members off.

When the ten minutes were up, Yihwan picked up his guitar again and slung the strap over his shoulders. "Japanese medley this time," he said, nodding at Steven. "*Seasons*, then *Maybe Not Today*, and then *Stage Fright*."

"You mean *Seasons*, and then *Terrified*, right?" Steven waved an annotated music sheet to remind him.

"Oh. Right..." Yihwan flashed the magnae a timid sideways glance. "What Steven said."

Fi was seated in the front row of the concert stadium, brows knitted together in concern. Even if Steven and Minchan didn't react to what could have been an indiscernible error, Fi was familiar enough with their repertoire to know Yihwan messed up on that medley.

Sighing, she sat back in her chair and watched the band as she mulled over another phone conversation she'd overheard inside the dressing room earlier. She didn't need to hear the voice on the other line to know who it was. His tone and body language gave him away.

For a moment, she toyed with the idea of calling that person to give her a piece of her mind.

"Stop. Stop, stop—" she heard Yihwan say over the microphone, and she stopped to look up at the stage warily, like she had been caught red-handed.

"I'm sorry, my bad," Yihwan said and motioned for Minchan to reconvene with Steven at the back.

With everyone's backs turned, Fi snuck a chance to tinker with Yihwan's phone, which he left in her care. A ten-second debate about personal privacy ran in her head before she finally went "Screw it," grabbed the phone, and looked through the band leader's contacts. By the time Yihwan called for a set repeat, Fi had already saved Han Haera's number on her phone.

It sat in her contact list for weeks.

Fi wasn't surprised Yihwan began to turn to the bottle. He started small—a few shots each day at the dorm or whichever hotel they were staying in—and eventually ended up inviting Steven, Minchan, and their staff for drinks night after every concert night.

She had seen this before, and back then she wished she'd never have to see it happen again.

Oh well, she thought. *You can't always get what you want.*

Because, of course, she wanted time alone with Yihwan like this: sitting side by side on the floor, backs against the side of the bed; his head on her shoulder, her hand on his cheek, musing about love and how it changed the people it touched.

A lovely image, but looks can be deceiving.

They were in Bangkok for Leap of Faith's third leg. Fi and Yihwan were alone in the band's hotel room after she decided to haul his wasted ass out of their after party. No one dared say anything to the band leader's face, but Fi saw the way Steven and Minchan had exchanged worried glances during Yihwan's nth toast tonight. His drinking had officially gotten out of control, all thanks, perhaps, to that single phone call he received from Han Haera the day before the tour kickoff.

"Are you sober now?"

"Little bit."

Fi raised two fingers in front of his face. Only the dimmed bedside lamps and the light down the hall leading to the bathroom illuminated the sprawling luxury suite, but she supposed this was a good test of sobriety anyhow. "How many?"

"Two pretty ones."

"Then my job here is done," she said as she made a move to stand up to put away the bowl of warm water by her feet, as well as the wet towel she used to wipe his face and neck earlier. He grabbed hold of her arm, a silent plea for her to stay.

She lifted her free hand to gently pat his cheek, her gaze on him pensive. His skin wasn't as flushed as it was when they unceremoniously left the party earlier, and that lessened her worries, if only a little. "You should sleep, Yihwan. We're not getting on a plane until later in the afternoon but—"

"Why do you think she left me, Fi?"

"Yihwan-ah."

"No... tell me. You saw us together, Haera and I. You must have seen *something*."

She *had* seen them, true. But Fi never looked for signs, for cracks beneath the delicate crystal that was Yihwan's precious love affair. All she saw was the love she could never have.

"I don't know what you want me to say."

Tears began to make Yihwan's eyes sparkle even more, and Fi mustered up all the courage she had to keep herself from looking away. They say that a heart breaking creates no sound, and Fi had always counted on that whenever faced with situations such as this.

"I was doing fine, right?" he asked, quick to wipe tears away with the back of his hand. "We worked like hell day in and day out in Japan—and I forgot all about her. I was okay! Even when she announced that she was dating that…that hotshot—"

"Jung Hwichan."

"Whatever."

He let go of her arm so he can bury his face in his palms and breathe, his posture reminding Fi of his reaction the day Han Haera's announcement made the news. In front of his band members, he'd acted cool, shrugging in response to the *Are-you-okays*. But she caught him sitting alone in the corridor of their rehearsal studio in Japan, head buried in his palms, humming something random she thought he might have heard on the radio.

As it turned out, the tune was something Yihwan came up with until it grew verses, a refrain, a chorus, a bridge. His heartbreak over Haera finding someone new bled through *Maybe Not Today*, the most popular track off EG Project's first Japanese album.

"Everything will be fine, you'll see" was all she can offer as consolation at the moment. It was all she could offer herself through three years of silently loving him, after all.

He scoffed, as though insulted by how much Fi has downplayed the situation. "If you were in my shoes, I doubt you'd be able to say the same thing."

Something inside her froze, then burned like wildfire, angry heat rushing to her cheeks. She felt compelled to slap him, but held herself back. If Jo Yihwan's face showed up swollen in airport pictures later, it wouldn't be because his enraged road manager decided to smack him around for an ill-timed comment.

"You're lucky…" Fi said, her hands balled fists against the carpet. "At the very least, Haera loved you back. It was brief, but I imagine it's a million times better than pining for someone who's always looking the other way."

The look on Yihwan's face turned curious. "That... happened to you?"

Now it was her turn to scoff. And perhaps it was because she still had a bit of liquid courage left in her system that she allowed the words to escape her. "See? You were so busy looking at her, you wouldn't even spare a glance *for me*."

Staring at his face, Fi could almost see the words she uttered slowly sinking into Yihwan's psyche. She saw it in the flicker in his eyes, the slackening of his jaw.

He looked at her now as if he was seeing her for the first time. Unable to hold his gaze, Fi looked away. But the moment tears started drawing paths down her cheeks, Yihwan took her in his arms and whispered apologies that melded with her quiet sobs.

Silence blanketed the room for a long while. As Fi let herself be held by Yihwan, the wheels in her head worked overtime. *What now? What do I say next?* She never imagined telling Yihwan of her feelings like this. Heck, she never had any plans of confessing them at all. For a moment, she wished she could turn back time so she could leave the room with her shattered heart still hidden from view.

She decided it was time to really leave, but he refused to let her go so easily. Closing her eyes for a second, she felt the pad of his thumb against her cheekbone, wiping away a tear. When she took in her next breath, his fingers were in her hair, and her vision of him blurred as he leaned in for a kiss.

Fi took a deep breath. *This is it.*

And then, it wasn't.

Text Log: Jo Yihwan & Filipina Legaspi
August 5

> Yihwan, 10:47 am
> Are you awake?

Fi, 10:50 am
Now I am. Good morning, Yihwan.

> Yihwan, 10:54 am
> I'm so sorry about last night. ;n;
> You can keep the shirt, and I'll have yours cleaned up ASAP,
> I promise. I really am so sorry.
> I don't even know what got into me. ;o;

Fi, 10:58 am
Don't worry about it. Hey, it's almost 11.
Did you guys have breakfast?

> Yihwan, 11:05 am
> We had it brought up. Minchan ate everything.

Fi, 11:07 am
Shocking.

> Yihwan, 11:40 am
> Fi...I really am so sorry.
> And not just about what I'd tried to do.

Fi, 11:45 am
I'll feel even worse if you keep apologizing like that.
Let's just pretend I never said anything, okay?

> Yihwan, 12:01 pm
> Thing is, I'm very bad at pretending.

Fi, 12:04 pm
I'll give you lessons for a new pair of jeans.

TRACK FIVE

Scrutiny, Mutiny

I T WAS STRANGE how calm she was about this.

Fi was still in bed, scrolling through her text exchange with Yihwan. Somehow, she felt confident she could face the band leader today without the need to avert his gaze, unlike the time she couldn't even look into his eyes for more than three seconds.

The truth will set you free, they said, and she supposed that today, those words held true.

Because the ball was in Yihwan's court now, and though she's still undecided if she wanted him to do something about it, she relished the feeling of relief in her chest.

She closed her eyes and recalled the moment he almost kissed her. But the alcohol in his system said, "Not today" and forced him to hurl. All over her shirt.

She remembered sitting still, eyes shut and anticipating her lips coming to contact with his, but it wasn't disappointment she felt when warmth spread all over her shirt instead. It was concern (maybe a bit of panic and a dash of disgust) that she felt for Yihwan, who was too embarrassed to do anything but help her clean up, go through his wardrobe, and find something else for her to wear.

Fi smiled. Last night was definitely still memorable.

Her eyelids fluttered open when she heard her phone ring.

Gabriel Park
CALLING…

"Hey, Gabe."

"Hm. That tone. I suppose you haven't seen the thing yet."

"What thing?"

"Where are you?"

She sat up and scanned the room for her laptop. "What thing?" she asked again, hopping off the bed to grab the device and do a quick search. If it's Gabriel calling, it was highly likely some damage control needed to be done.

"A blind item. A very obvious one. Were you in the band's hotel room last night?"

"Yeah, Yihwan got himself sick drinking."

"Shit."

Upon hearing the mild expletive, Fi imagined Gabriel standing by his desk, palm pressed against his face, fingers possibly massaging his temples. His was a job that required quick thinking and a whole lot of patience, and if the vague detail he just blurted out was anything to go by, she'd bet he was troubleshooting another EG Project issue.

An issue that involved her.

She found out exactly what when she pulled up the search returns and saw a *Dispatch* article containing photos of a man and a woman against a familiar milieu. The faces have been blurred, sure, but Fi's hands turned cold when she finally grasped the gravity of the situation.

Top Idol Sleeps with a Woman in Foreign Hotel, the blind item headline read.

This time, she was the one who wanted to throw up.

Back in Seoul, Gabriel watched helplessly as a PR disaster exploded right in front of his very eyes. They haven't even recovered from the entire Han Haera brouhaha yet, and now they had a new fire to extinguish. Part of him wanted to yell at Fi over the phone for being so careless, but he knew it could have been any female member of the band's entourage just doing their job, and nothing would have changed.

"The fans already know it's Yihwan," one of the younger PR managers voiced out. "Subtlety isn't exactly in *Dispatch*'s vocabulary."

Gabriel sighed. "What time does EGP leave Bangkok?"

"Five o' clock, Manila-bound."

Manila. He recalled how thrilled Fi was about this trip when the tour itinerary was decided. It was five years ago when Fi finished a short film and music course at an Amethyst-affiliated school and received a job offer at the company. Still young and impressionable, she took the offer, not yet fully realizing that the nature of her job would steal many opportunities to fly back home.

If memory served him right, Fi's last vacation was three years ago. Now Gabriel felt concerned she might get pulled out of the Manila leg because of this morning's developments.

So far, however, none of the higher-ups have said anything about replacing her.

"How many hours from Seoul to Manila?" he asked.

"Four hours, give or take."

Minja peered at him through her glasses. "Don't tell me you're actually flying to Manila."

Gabriel shut down his laptop and cleared his desk, contemplating how to justify the sudden want to accompany the band while they navigated through this mess. If he flew out within the next two hours, he might even get to Manila before they do.

Minja spoke up again. "You do know you can troubleshoot things from here, right? We have this thing called *technology*."

There really was no use concealing something Minja already sniffed out of him a long time ago, so he decided to say, "Fi needs me."

The woman went "Ah," like the answer had been obvious all along. "I think the more accurate reply would be "'Fi *might* need me.'"

"Doesn't matter. I should be there."

Suvarnabhumi Airport bustled with activity on a daily basis, but it threatened to burst at the seams whenever celebrities arrived in and left the country. Throngs of avid fans and press people gathered at the concourse to welcome them or send them off, and security was tripled so that no untoward incidents happen.

The scene at the airport today was similar to what the band saw during their arrival two days ago, although the air was now rife with tension. Over the past several hours, a lot of speculation about the *Dispatch* blind item came up. Many fans and netizens have concluded that it was, in fact, Jo Yihwan and one of EG Project's female entourage members who were photographed at the hotel.

The fans were enraged. They wanted to know who exactly the woman was and why she was wearing the band leader's shirt when she left the hotel suite they entered together.

"Don't be scared, noona. We have your back," Minchan reassured the roadie as they prepared to step out of their van.

But Fi's mind was already somewhere else. Home. The prospect of coming home after five years was enough to give her courage and just go, mob of angry fans nothwithstanding.

"I'm not scared." *Fear is for people who do bad things*, her late father once told her. She was then six years old, hiding under the bed because her school uniform got soiled after a classmate pushed her while playing tag. *You didn't do anything wrong. And we can always wash your clothes.*

She repeated the words in her head with conviction, her father's voice so clear, it was as though he was right there with her.

I didn't do anything wrong. Among other things, it was her responsibility to make sure every member of the band was in tip-top shape or well taken care of should they not be in the best of health.

Heart pounding against her rib cage, Fi stepped out of the van right behind the band. The walk spanning several meters to the airport lobby felt like miles, and the screaming fans that usually made her smile now made her insides turn.

Her knees were like jelly as they walked through the concourse. A blur of fan signs and placards being waved up in the air came to view, as well as fans who reached over the barricades to hand out flowers or gifts. Airport security handled them and turned them over to the band's bodyguards. On the way to the immigration desk, Fi kept her head down and tried her best to keep up with the rest of the entourage.

As the immigration officer checked her documents, Fi gave her group an uneasy sideways glance, feeling like they've gone ahead without her. They haven't; it was only her paranoia talking.

Once she crossed the threshold to the boarding area, Fi let out a breath of relief and almost skipped toward her pack. She saw Yihwan look back and smile at her. He seemed relieved too.

But her relief turned to mild confusion when Yihwan did a double take, turned on his heel, and started toward her. She belatedly registered screaming behind her and looked back, only to have her hair grabbed with such strong force that it threw her off balance.

A second later, everything went black.

[BLIND ITEM] Top Idol Sleeps with a Woman in a Foreign Hotel
August 5 | Dispatch

Top Idol A was recently photographed bringing a woman into his band's hotel suite after an overseas concert. Both Idol A and the woman had reportedly been drinking with the rest of Idol A's bandmates and staff but left the restaurant in the middle of a victory party.

According to the hotel staff, Idol A returned to the hotel past midnight, together with the woman in the photograph. Hours later, the woman emerged from the suite wearing a different set of clothes, all allegedly Idol A's.

Idol A's agency must be scratching their heads over this, especially since the very same idol had just been cleared from a huge dating rumor.

[EMBEDDED PHOTOS]

COMMENTS

[+5,620, -967] The only idols on tour right now are EG Project and NCore. I'd bet my money on EGP's Steven Bae, but the profile doesn't seem to match. If we go by body build alone, I'd say this is Jo Yihwan. Guess it really isn't true that he's dating Han Haera after all.

[+2,065, -692] I've been to Thailand before, and this hotel exterior is DEFINITELY The Siam. My friends who are EG Project stans told me they're in Thailand for a tour, so this is definitely an EG Project member.

[+1,389, -912] I feel so betrayed, Jo Yihwan. That shirt is a fan gift and you just gave it to a woman you slept with? Disgusting.

[+1,118, -798] Why is everyone so sure it's Jo Yihwan? It could be their magnae. Didn't he say in one interview that he likes foreign women? Congrats on the sex, Song Minchan. You are now a man.

[+967, -423] My YiVen heart is crushed.

TRACK SIX

MISS & HIT

"**D**O YOU KNOW you've been making that face every time you look at me?" Fi asked Gabriel, who kept cringing at the sight of the long scratch across her left cheekbone. "I feel like I've turned into a hideous witch or something."

"No. I'm sorry. When I see that scratch on your face I start getting irrationally angry."

It was past midnight, four hours since EG Project landed in Manila and found Gabriel at the airport waiting for them. Fi was surprised to see him there, barking orders at the male members of the band's entourage. The most logical explanation, she thought, was that Amethyst gave him the green light to call the shots.

It wasn't unheard of. Gabriel's department was in charge of making sure the band stayed the pretty package they're sold as, and the trio *did* need a little debriefing after the incident at Suvarnabhumi.

As did she.

"It's only a scratch."

"Steven said you fell on the floor. You were unconscious for a bit. We should get your head checked to—"

"—see how stupid I've been? I think we both know the answer to that."

"I'm not kidding, Fi."

She narrowed her eyes at the man, gauging his current mood. Gabriel usually found humor in things that should be regarded seriously, but today seemed like an exception. She was about to tell him to *chill*, but the sight of her mother approaching the dining table effectively stole her words. Fi was still unable to wrap her head around the fact that she was home. Growing up, she had never been away from home longer than three days, and yet

34

somehow she managed to survive five years in South Korea on her own.

"I hope you take instant coffee, Gabriel."

"Oh, of course." Gabriel smiled at Fi's mother, Diana Legaspi, who placed a cup of coffee on the table in front of him. "This cup is so much bigger than vendo cups, so that's just great."

Diana smiled back at him and lingered by the table to ruffle her daughter's hair. Fi, in turn, was quick to wrap her arms around her mother's waist.

Gabriel enjoyed a sip of his coffee and watched mother and daughter dote on each other for the next ten seconds. He apologized for crashing in for the night—"For the next couple of nights," Fi corrected—and Diana simply dismissed him with a wave of her hand.

"You kids stay here while I prepare your beds," Diana said. Fi offered to help, but her mother insisted she stay with their guest. There was a mischievous glint in her mother's eyes that Fi instantly recognized; she'd seen this before whenever her high school friend Carlos would visit their house for school-related activities. "I won't take long. I'm sure you've had a long day..."

Fi shook her head once her mother turned away, only then noticing how Gabriel was staring at her with an amused look on his face.

"You guys are cute," he said, the smile on his face still there. "Actually, everything in this house is." He raised the cup in which Diana served him coffee. It was one of those magic mugs, designed to reveal pictures on the surface when hot water got poured into it. Gabriel's cup had Shinhwa Eric's face plastered on it.

"Oh god, of all the things!" Fi exclaimed at the sight, hand flying to her mouth as she laughed.

"Never pegged you as a Shinhwa fan."

"That's my ate's."

"Hm?"

"Big sister."

"Right."

Gabriel didn't seem to believe her, and she was ready to prove him wrong, but her phone hummed against the wooden table. It was a message from Yihwan.

Are you home? Settled in for the night?

Fi left the message unanswered, wanting Yihwan to believe that they had, indeed, retired for the night. She refused to engage in a conversation—albeit in short messaging format—with the band leader just then, especially after the heated argument they all had regarding her living arrangements while EG Project was in Manila.

Through Gabriel, the band and Fi were informed that Amethyst wanted Fi to stay in a different hotel to prevent further speculation about the woman in the blind item. But while the band thought the decree unfair to their road manager, Fi was perfectly fine with it, saying she knew exactly where she wanted to stay. She had a home here, after all, and no hotel room would ever be as comforting as her own.

Fi never expected the boys to react so violently over the matter. Of course it was touching to see them stand up for her, but she decided she didn't need any more stress after the Suvarnabhumi incident. She didn't even argue with Gabriel when he declared he'd be staying with her to make sure she was safe. The day already felt like it had gone on forever. She really just wanted to go home.

And now that she was here, she felt compelled to shut the entire universe out of her system for at least a few hours.

She switched her phone off.

With a groan, Yihwan tossed and turned in his bed. In the last half hour, he'd sent Fi five messages, but she hadn't replied to any of them. He wondered out loud if the local SIM cards they were provided with earlier actually worked.

"Hyung, she's probably already asleep," Minchan said.

"I just feel so bad about what happened," Yihwan replied, raising his voice slightly so he could be heard over Steven's snoring. "I wish I could have done something to protect her. I wanted to keep her close, but Gabriel..."

"Gabriel hyung had a point, y'know. If the fans see her around here, they'll put two and two together, and who knows what's going to happen next?"

The band leader buried his head against a pillow and groaned. Why was nothing going his way lately?

"What really happened back there, anyway?" Minchan asked. None of them questioned Fi's presence in the paparazzi photos because they knew why she took Yihwan back to the hotel that night. But Fi *was* wearing Yihwan's clothes when she left the suite, and that was a critical detail. "Did you and Fi noona...you know...?"

"Are you insane?" Yihwan snapped, in a manner that could perhaps be misconstrued as defensive.

"That's what the blind items are saying. I'm just clearing it up."

"Nothing happened. I was drunk, she took care of me, and I..." Yihwan winced at the memory. "I vomited all over her clothes."

"Seriously? That's disgusting."

"Tell me about it."

"You puked on noona's clothes, and *she* gets cursed at by the entire fandom." Minchan shook his head. "This must be your lucky year."

The moment Fi opened the door to her sister's bedroom, Gabriel let out a "Wow." Three times. She let him take *everything* in before giving him a walkthrough.

It's the walls he noticed first. They were wallpapered with posters of various KPop acts, most of them first-generation idols of the late 90s, like g.o.d., H.O.T., and Shinhwa. Albums were neatly stacked together on a two-tier bookshelf by the window, but somehow Gabriel felt like the room had not been lived in for a while.

"Where's your sister?"

"Overseas, not sure exactly where at the moment."

He looked at her, waited for her to say something more.

"She's on a quest to save the world, one starving child at a time."

His brows creased as he crossed the threshold and laid his coat on the bed. Fi shrugged. "Social work."

"Oh. Wow, that's great. You must be proud of her."

"All the time," she said. "I wish she'd call more often though."

"Would you be able to answer if she did?"

A pause. "Touché. Anyway…I'm sorry about the sheets. I guess these are the most gender-neutral ones mom could find."

"It's perfectly fine. Purple's totally my color, see?" Gabriel held a purple pillow to his cheek and batted his eyelashes. "Perfect for my skin tone."

Fi let out an obnoxious cackle, but shut up a second later. It was the wee hours of the morning after all, and the neighbors were asleep. She then showed Gabriel where the light switch was, the electric fan, and the power outlets, and the hall that led to the second-floor bathroom before saying goodnight.

"Sleep well, Fi," he said as she walked out the door.

"You too. We have a busy day ahead of us."

The weather was as humid as Manila can get, but Fi woke up feeling like she just had the best sleep in years, even after she was jolted awake at 4:00 a.m. because the neighbor's roosters were cock-a-doodle-dooing like nobody's business. She missed that. She even missed the sound of tricycles roaring by.

She checked her phone for the time: 11:00 a.m. It was too late for breakfast, but there was no mistaking the smell of tocino being cooked downstairs. Still half-awake, she got out of bed and shuffled to the bathroom. But before she could twist the door knob, the door swung open, revealing Gabriel wearing only a towel around his waist.

"Hey, good morning."

The sight confused her, and yet she couldn't bring herself to look away.

What in the world is Gabe doing at my house in a—oh, right, he's staying for... a couple of days. How is it possible that his chest looks like this?

She never imagined that the toned body existed underneath Gabriel's usual office attire. To be more precise, she never imagined his body until...okay, well, that moment.

"Fi?"

She was wide awake now, thanks to the smell of his soap—or was that aftershave?—and she looked up at Gabriel when he called her name. Droplets of water at the tips of his long lashes distracted her from his smile for a second. "Yeah?"

He held her by the shoulders ("Hey, what are you doing?" she almost yelled, crossing her arms over her chest) and gently shoved her to the side so he can step out of the bathroom and into the corridor. Embarrassed by her train of thought, Fi cleared her throat and mumbled, "There's br—er, lunch downstairs," before rushing into the bathroom and shutting the door behind her loudly.

"Well, hurry downstairs then. Let's have *'br—er, lunch'* together."

So strange, she thought, as she took in a deep breath and pressed a hand to her chest to calm her heart. Fi certainly wasn't new to this kind of...*display*. AmEnt's male models and trainees often sauntered from one rehearsal room to another in only their jeans. She had even seen all of EG Project shirtless and in their boxer shorts during backstage costume changes. Seeing Gabriel without a shirt on shouldn't be so different.

So why did it feel like she'd just run a mile?

It took her a while to shake the glorious vision out of her head. And when she finally did, she somehow ended up fussing over how her hair should look. Or if she should change into something other than her floral pajamas and worn-out high school P.E. shirt.

Come on, Filipina. It's just Gabriel, she told herself, and decided to tie her hair up in a neat ponytail. She didn't bother changing into something else either and found herself silly for even considering it. She did wash her face and brush her teeth twice, though.

Coming down the stairs, Fi was surprised to see a familiar face in the living room. She squealed and tackle-hugged her friend, Carlos.

"'Tang ina, na-miss kita, ah!" Carlos exclaimed after a long, drawn-out hug. They bickered all the way to the dining area where Gabriel was waiting, stopping only so that Fi can introduce them.

"Gabe, this is Carlos, a good friend of mine from high school."

Carlos placed the bilao he brought on the table, wiped his hand against his jeans, and offered Gabriel a handshake.

"And this is Gabriel, our PR guy."

They shook hands, and Fi invited Carlos to have lunch with them. Carlos clicked his tongue. "Sorry, I have to go back to school in a bit. You're not the only one who has a job now, Fi."

"Right! You're a guidance counselor now!"

"Yep. I just came down here to bring you your favorite kutsinta because Tita said you were coming home."

Touched, Fi smiled at her friend and stepped forward to hug him again. "Aww, mahal mo talaga ako," she said.

"May bayad 'yan, uy."

NEWS REPORT
Channel 8
August 5 | Manila, Philippines

[Establishing shot of international airport, followed by video footage of screaming fans holding up signs while East Genesis Project walks through concourse]

CAPTION: South Korean pop-rock band East Genesis Project arrives for Manila leg of Leap of Faith tour

ELISE BONIFACIO: Fans of the popular South Korean pop-rock band East Genesis Project flocked to the NAIA Terminal 3 last night to welcome the band as they landed in Manila for their upcoming two-day concert. FilOriginals, as the Philippine-based fans are called, surprised the band members by singing a song off their second album as they walked through the airport.

[Video footage of fans singing *7:45 AM*, and the band members stopping to listen, waving and bowing to the fans present.]

[Video clip of Jo Yihwan]

CAPTION: Jo Yihwan, East Genesis Project guitarist and band leader

JO YIHWAN: (English subs on screen) I think it's the first time we've ever experienced this kind of welcome while on tour... and we are all very thankful for the effort and love the Filipino fans have shown so far.

ELISE BONIFACIO: (off-screen) Please share a message for all your Filipino fans who are looking forward to your concert.

41

JO YIHWAN: (English subs on screen) Mabuhay, Philippines! Thanks so much for the warm welcome. We have an awesome show prepared for all of you, and we hope to see you all there!

[Video footage of EG Project members taking time to shake hands and receive gifts from fans as they walk out of the airport.]

ELISE BONIFACIO: Meanwhile, Jump Productions has announced that tickets are already sold out for the EG Project concert happening on August 8 and 9 at the Baywalk Concert Grounds, further proof of the band's massive popularity in the country.

Elise Bonifacio, Channel 8 News.

TRACK SEVEN

TAKE A STEP BACK

YIHWAN WAS THROWN COMPLETELY OFF BALANCE when, instead of Fi, senior road manager Justin Hong arrived at technical rehearsal the next day.

"Hyung. Are they pulling Fi out of the tour?"

"I'm not really sure. Amethyst just sent me here. Emergency deployment."

Confused, Yihwan frowned. Didn't Fi just call them a while ago to make sure they were on the way to rehearsal? She said nothing about not showing up or having someone replace her.

She obviously didn't know about this new development.

But the band leader knew he would achieve nothing by directing his anger at their newly appointed road manager, so he tried to stay calm even though he was itching to make a phone call to Seoul. He'd led Justin backstage and handed over several things—a concert setlist, a schedule of activities, a directory of numbers to call—all of them previously organized by Fi.

Justin had given the documents a look-see and told Yihwan to go ahead and get back to rehearsal. "I'll handle this. Don't worry."

But Yihwan wasn't worried about Justin, not at all. He had more years of road manager experience than Fi, and the band leader trusted his judgment enough to leave logistical concerns in his hands. What nagged at him was the possibility that Fi was—or will be—completely pulled from the tour. Amethyst better not be thinking it.

Were they?

Riding a hot, cramped jeepney wasn't exactly Fi's idea of fun, but watching Gabriel's facial expressions whenever he saw or heard anything relatively shocking—a random passenger suddenly passing him coins, or the startling, reverberating laughter that's actually another jeepney's horn—turned out to be so amusing. She tried her hardest not to laugh at him at first, afraid he might feel offended, but in the end she couldn't help but let out a giggle.

He was just too cute.

And maybe Gabriel was trying hard as well, Fi concluded. Only, his intent seemed to be to placate her after an AmEnt higher-up called to temporarily relieve her of road manager duties.

"Won't you show me around instead? I've never been to Manila before," he said, wearing a smile so earnest she didn't have the heart to say no.

So they went to Intramuros, where Fi casually filled Gabriel in on the history of the place: how the walled city *was* Manila and the seat of government during the Spanish era, and how its location was ideal for the Manila-Acapulco galleon trade back then.

They took a walking tour, and she noticed how quickly he was captivated by the architecture. She watched as he lingered at certain spots, admiring what was left of the original structures as well as the newer installations.

"This is beautiful, Fi. There's so much history in here."

"Oh, there's more. We're only in Fort Santiago," Fi said, raising her phone up in the air to take a candid shot of Gabriel appreciating the view. She took a perfect silhouetted shot of him the first time—back to her, both hands on his hips, gazing at Plaza Moriones almost contemplatively—but he put a damper on her second attempt when he suddenly turned around and asked what she was doing.

"Documentation, of course."

Gabriel shook his head. "If you really want to document this day in photographs, you should be in them too."

"You're the tourist here." *Snap. Snap.* She captured him walking toward her and reaching for the phone in her hand. Before she could protest, Gabriel snatched it away and raised it in front of them for a selfie.

"Okay, here we go." He bent his knees a little and wrapped an arm over her shoulder, and he was *soclose* to her that she got a whiff of his scent once more as he counted: "One, two, Fi!"

"Did you just say 'Fi'?" she asked as he checked the gallery to see if the photo came out all right.

"Yeah."

She snorted.

"What? Your name makes me smile."

Her heart skipped a beat, delaying her attempt at a witty comeback for a good three seconds. "Remind me to get some pizza so we'll have something to put all that cheese on."

"Awesome. I *love* pizza!" Gabriel laughed, and it was as infectious as it was deadly, making Fi's heart do leaps and somersaults and things she really couldn't allow herself to feel at the moment.

"Come on. The park's closing in a few hours, and we haven't even made a dent in the itinerary yet." She took her phone from his hands and, with quick strides, walked ahead of Gabriel, a feeble attempt to keep herself from staring at him too long.

"There's always tomorrow. Or the next day."

She stopped in her tracks and turned to look at him. "Aren't you here for work?"

"I *am* working."

"No, you're not. You're playing hooky."

Gabriel caught up with her. "I'm keeping you company. And away from the band."

"I can do that on my own."

"Really? *Can* you?"

She frowned at him, not because of the insinuation he made, but because the insinuation was accurate. If Yihwan called her right now, Fi wasn't sure she could resist. *Like a moth to a flame*, as Gabriel himself had put it.

Gabriel didn't get an answer. Instead, Fi spun on her heel and made her way through Plaza Moriones with quicker, heavier steps.

Jesus, Gabe. How could you be so insensitive?

Cursing under his breath, Gabriel ran after Fi, holding on to her wrist when he finally caught up with her. But she turned around and looked at him with eyes that glistened with tears and all the words he meant to say just flew out the window. For a passing moment, he was transported back to the first time this sight presented itself to him.

It was on the day she told him, over soju and makgeolli, that she had fallen in love with Jo Yihwan. That she hadn't been aware how the feeling sort of crept up from behind, took her heart hostage, and refused to let go.

"I'm sorry," he managed to say, the words coming out like a sigh. "I know how much the band means to you. Now is just not the best time."

Gabriel knew he didn't need to say anything more. Fi was smart and seasoned enough to understand the repercussions of being seen with the band when hostile fangirls are out for blood.

A tiny ache gnawed at his heart when Fi pried his hand off her wrist. With reluctance, he let her go.

"It's just a little off-putting, is all," she finally spoke after a few seconds of awkward silence. "This has been my life for the past four years—being with the band everywhere they went and generally being part of their daily lives. Now it feels like I've been shut out, like I've been disowned by my own family."

Gabriel sighed and looked away, directing his gaze toward an old structure somewhere in the distance. It wasn't the best time to wax poetic about how beautiful Fi's eyes were, even if only at the back of his mind. It's those goddamn tears. Why did they have to make her eyes sparkle like that?

"It's just a strange feeling, to be home and still feel so lost."

He failed to come up with a response to that.

"I think it's going to rain," she mumbled and looked up at the sky, and Gabriel knew she was only trying her best to keep her tears in.

46

Again, he reached for her, making sure his slender fingers wrapped gently around her wrist. She smiled, and all of a sudden a weight was lifted off his chest. Fi gave him a tug and he yielded, wondering if she had any idea how much power she had over him at that moment.

At *any* moment.

―――――――

"But are you feeling all right?"

"Yes. *Yes*, I've told you a hundred times."

"I know your knack for understating things, is all. Where are you anyway?"

"Intramuros."

"*Ohhh*kay."

Fi was sitting by the steps of the Manila Cathedral, one of the oldest churches in Manila and the venue for papal masses in the country, waiting for Gabriel to return. It's already been fifteen minutes since he wandered off to buy bottled water, and he still had not returned. "Carl, I'll talk to you later. I feel like my towering tourist has gotten lost and might be trying to call me," she told her friend, who just laughed at the possible predicament and promptly agreed to end the call.

She got up and turned toward the intricately carved cathedral doors—bronze, beautiful, and sadly, closed. It was a weekday, when masses ended as early as one in the afternoon. Looking up at the arches of the sacred structure, Fi momentarily closed her eyes to say a silent prayer of thanks and supplication. Seconds later, she heard a steady clopping sound against concrete, *and* a voice she could recognize anywhere.

"Fi! Look what I found!"

"You said you'd just be buying bottled water!" she exclaimed, running down the steps just as a red-and-silver calesa stopped right in front of her.

Gabriel was all smiles when he raised two water bottles, one in each hand, for her to see. "Come up," he said, freeing his hands so he can hold them out to assist her.

She smiled, amused. "Are you serious?"

He jerked an eyebrow upward and tilted his head, and Fi was almost inclined to tell him off for acting like a puppy when he was over six feet tall. Instead, she took his hand and got on the calesa, its shaky build causing her to trip on a step and fall face first against Gabriel's chest.

"Whoa there, careful," he said, one hand holding hers, the other grasping her shoulder.

Dear God, he smells so good.

Wait—what? Fi scrambled to get a hold of herself but managed to squeeze her face even more against the PR manager's chest. Blood rushed to her face even more when she heard him chuckle.

"All right, here we go. Nice and easy." His strong hands steadied her until she was able to control her body parts again and sit properly beside him, the smallness of the carriage forcing them to squeeze against each other. He handed her a water bottle. "You okay?"

"Yeah." *No, not really. How is it possible for you to smell this...nice? We've been walking around for hours in this heat!*

"What about the band?" he asked. The cochero-slash-tour guide proceeded to lead them out of Plaza Roma and onto General Luna Street, passing by more long-standing structures that now housed more modern establishments such as offices, restaurants, and even souvenir shops.

"What about them?"

"I thought I saw you talking on the phone as we were rounding the corner," Gabriel pointed out, taking the water bottle from her again and twisting the cap off for her. "Weren't you checking in on them?"

"No. I was talking to Carlos."

"Oh. I thought you were talking to Yihwan."

Fi shook her head and decided to just roll the cool plastic bottle between her palms, afraid that she might choke if she started drinking *right here, right now.* "They're probably still at tech. God,

I hope the equipment Jump Productions provided them isn't shitty," she said, recalling a recent report that another KPop act complained about having so many technical problems during their showcase in Manila. "Minchan hates it when the acoustics don't sound right."

"Only Minchan?"

"Yihwan and Steven too, of course. But Yihwan is very diplomatic with these things, and Steven can be too lazy to actually speak up. But Minchan... oh, if looks could kill."

"So your friend Carlos..."

"Hm?"

"You look...*comfortable*."

Fi's brows furrowed a bit when she looked at Gabriel, wondering if she heard him right. The only other time she had heard this tone from someone was when petty jealousy prompted Yihwan to ask Haera about her male co-stars.

Don't be ridiculous, Fi. Why would Gabriel be jealous?

She only shrugged and twisted her bottle cap open. "He's a childhood friend, a high school and college batch mate." A sigh. "Also...my biggest *What If*."

"'What if'?"

"You know, the person who makes you wonder 'What if I'd told him about how I felt?' or 'What if we ended up together?' or 'What if we kissed?' That kind of person."

"I'm guessing you never told him."

The way she took a swig of water made it seem like she was having something alcoholic, and she laughed, saying, "That's not the kind of person I am."

"Then what kind are you?"

Fi turned to him with narrowed eyes. "*You* of all people should know."

"Spell it out for me here, Filipina. I don't want to assume things."

Laughter spilled out of her. Thank god for Gabriel. She didn't know what it was, but she had always found it easy to open up to him, somehow. With Gabriel, she felt...safe.

"I'm the kind who'd rather suffer in silence than be loudly rejected by the person I like."

"Ah." He nodded and took a drink of water as well. Teasing her a bit, he raised his bottle for a toast and she played along. They ended up laughing, but at the back of her mind, she thought of the night she confessed her feelings to Yihwan and his reaction to the revelation.

It was odd how that moment felt so far away now.

"It's so weird."

"What is?"

"I thought I'd moved on," she mumbled, her tone soft and almost as if she was embarrassed by what she was about to say. "I had Yihwan beside me every day. We talked, had meals, organized things for the band. We sat together almost *everywhere*. I thought I'd become immune. But that damned thing about him and Haera *had* to resurface, and it's difficult to watch him break again."

When she turned to look at Gabriel once more, Fi was briefly taken aback to see him gazing at her with the most attentive pair of brown eyes. For a second, she lost her train of thought, and she averted his gaze, taking another sip of water instead.

"So you're saying the feelings are back?"

She shook her head. "You know what? I'm not even sure how I feel anymore."

FROM JO YIHWAN'S KAKAOSTORY FEED

Filipina Legaspi
2 hours ago (12 hearts, 5 comments)

I'm surprised I was able to convince Gabe to eat all these! Please don't get a stomachache tonight.

-With Gabriel
(Photo attachment: Gabriel, grinning like an idiot, holding a plastic cup with sticks of isaw in it in one hand and a balut in the other.)

Gabriel Park
3 hours ago (15 hearts, 10 comments)

Plaza Moriones, Intramuros, Manila.
Didn't need to look very far to find something so beautiful.

-With Filipina

(Photo attachment: A shot of Manila Cathedral from a distance, with Fi standing at the steps, looking up at something.)

Steven Bae
5 hours ago (2,800 hearts, 302 comments)

Soundcheck, MNL Leg.

-With Yihwan & Minchan

(Photo attachment: A black-and-white photo of Yihwan and Minchan with their backs to him, taken from his spot behind the drumset.)

Song Minchan
5 hours ago (1,404 hearts, 378 comments)

Manila is as warm as the love you've shown us so far. See you on Saturday, FilOriginals!

TRACK EIGHT
WIND, MEET CAUTION

"**H**YUNG, shouldn't you be staying off the internet?"

Yihwan ignored Steven, who, in his opinion, didn't have the right to call him out on spending a lot of time online. The drummer had been very fanservice-y that afternoon during technical rehearsal, posting photos here and there on his Twitter and KakaoStory accounts. He had even replied to a few comments, something he didn't usually do.

But Yihwan also knew it was Damage Control à la Steven Bae, which followed the logic that fangirls would be willing to overlook certain things as long as they're happy.

"Hyung…"

Yihwan's eyes were fixed on two Kakaostory entries posted one after the other. *Someone seemed to have had a nice afternoon*, he thought. All while he was worried about how Fi could have taken the news of her temporary suspension. All while he was thinking about how all of this had been unfair to her.

He narrowed his eyes on the picture of Gabriel attached to Fi's post and felt the urge to wipe that smile off the PR manager's face with his fist.

Whoa.

Whoa there, Jo Yihwan.

Where did that come from?

He took a deep breath, and somehow he heard a buzzing in his ear. Buzzing that soon turned into Steven's voice.

"Hyung, are you with us?"

Yihwan looked up to see Steven and Minchan staring at him curiously. "What?"

"It's the fans," Minchan said, almost solemnly.

Still lost in his thoughts and swimming through an inexplicable wave of jea—wait, it could *not* be jealousy because *what even*— Yihwan stared dumbly at the magnae, waiting for an explanation.

"Photos of Fi noona are circulating now," the bassist offered, holding an iPad up for Yihwan to see the fan blog he had been looking at. "These are captures from some of our old airport photos. Some of them are photos taken at the Amethyst building. The fans are comparing her photos to the blurred one *Dispatch* published."

"It's only a matter of time until they put the pieces together," Steven declared. "Don't you think we should do something?"

They should, no question about that. But Yihwan had no idea how. That the internet had made things easier for this generation was an understatement, but it had also created monsters—faceless, disembodied creatures who seemed to have no agenda other than putting people down when they felt like it. They feasted on another person's misery and derived a sick sort of pride over someone else's disgrace.

And when the damage had been done, they would look for another unsuspecting victim and attack. It was a vicious cycle the band was all too familiar with; they just never realized the same thing would happen to them.

"We'll figure something out. I'm sure the management is on top of this too."

Thanks to the hard downpour brought in by an incoming typhoon, EG Project's schedules were cancelled the day before their Leap of Faith concert in Manila. Justin called Gabriel and the other AmEnt staff for an emergency meeting, leaving the band members to their own devices.

And while Steven and Minchan spent several hours playing games on their mobile phones, Yihwan resolved not to let Gabriel monopolize Fi's attention.

Not today, at least.

"Are you mad at me?" he asked Fi over the phone when she finally answered his call. "You haven't been taking my calls or replying to my messages since yesterday."

"Yihwan."

"Yes, that's my name."

"We both know what happened was a misstep. Mine and yours."

Some rumbling in the background—*a motorcyle, maybe?*—almost drowned out Fi's voice as she spoke. Yihwan also heard dogs barking every so often, and he thought perhaps her family owned a canine or two.

"I'm way past being mad at myself for letting this happen," she said. "I just want you guys to finish the Manila leg without any more incidents."

"Mianhae."

"What are you apologizing for?"

"Making your life difficult?"

"Stop that," she snapped. Yihwan could almost see the disapproving expression on Fi's face.

He paused, then said, "Let's meet up!"

"That's not possible."

"Well, that's unfair. You toured Gabriel hyung around that pretty place, and I get nothing?" *Congratulations, Jo Yihwan. You've just managed to sound like an extremely clingy son of a bitch*, he mused inwardly. He might not yet have completely grasped what his motivation were for acting like this, but he was certain of one thing at least: he needed to see Fi again.

Fi chuckled. "Even if I had the luxury of taking you guys somewhere, the weather's not going to make it fun. Don't you have that TV interview at Channel 8?"

"Cancelled. Today's a rest day."

"Oh. Get some rest, then."

"Bring me somewhere..."

"Did you just *whine*, Jo Yihwan?"

"That place you went to yesterday. Where is that?"

54

Intramuros, she told him. A historical landmark that's a jeepney ride away from her house. Ish. And then she started explaining to him what a jeepney was, to which he only replied with an "Mhm."

But really, the cogs in Yihwan's head were turning tirelessly as she continued talking about several other nice places to visit should the time, weather, or circumstance be convenient for them.

"Oh. Hey, Justin just sent me a message," he interrupted. "He's asking where you are right now because he needs to meet you for some kind of meeting but he doesn't have your number."

"Justin Hong? Is he my sub?"

"Yeah."

"Wow, you guys are lucky. He must not be busy with Silverazzi right now. But isn't he meeting Gabe today? I remember him sayi—"

"I don't know. Maybe they haven't met yet." There was a snippiness in Yihwan's tone, and he hoped Fi didn't detect it.

"Oh, all right. Well. I'm at home. Maybe we can meet somewhere nearby? The weather outside is still—"

"I'll tell him to come see you instead. What's your address?"

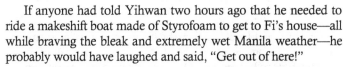

If anyone had told Yihwan two hours ago that he needed to ride a makeshift boat made of Styrofoam to get to Fi's house—all while braving the bleak and extremely wet Manila weather—he probably would have laughed and said, "Get out of here!"

And yet here he was, sitting on a plastic chair duct-taped on several slabs of Styrofoam attached together by, you guessed it, more duct tape. He was given a beach umbrella to protect himself from the rain when he got on, gingerly, about five minutes ago, and now he was holding it over his head. His eyes darted here and there, wary of people who might recognize him.

Them, actually, because Steven and Minchan were about two wades away. They got a bigger "styroboat," as the locals called it, which they enthusiastically shared. Yihwan looked over his shoulder and frowned behind the pulled-up collar of his hoodie, seeing his drummer and bassist fool around. They were reenacting that famous scene from *Titanic* and making their boatman as well as other passersby laugh. He was about to scold them when his boatman told him that they have reached their destination.

Yihwan stared at the structure, a stone house that looked like it had been standing there for a long time. A good third of it was now submerged in water, but the sturdy wooden plank bridging the entrance to a flight of stairs that led to a door was evidence of how its dwellers have acclimated to the flooding.

The band leader paid for his ride, as well as Steven and Minchan's. They all crossed the plank in their squishy shoes and found themselves in front of an old wooden door with a crucifix nailed to it. Yihwan knocked.

There was a fleeting look of horror on the face of the middle-aged woman who answered the door. Understandable, as all three of them were wearing dark-colored hoodies and black baseball caps pulled low over their faces.

"Hi. We're Fi's colleagues," Steven quickly offered after taking his cap off, perhaps to spare Yihwan from whipping out the broken English. "Is she home?"

The woman's eyes were fixed on them when she yelled "Filipina!" and it only took a few seconds for Fi to emerge from a door. Her eyes widened at the sight of them.

"Ho—ly. Shit. What are you all doing here? Where's Justin?"

"Noona!"

One by one, Fi grabbed them by the wrist and pulled them into the house before shutting the door. After a round of hasty introductions to her mother, Diana excitedly disappeared into the kitchen, insisting she was having some merienda prepared.

As soon as Diana left the room, Fi smacked Yihwan on the chest. "Jesus Christ, Yihwan. Neo micheosseo?"

"What? No one knows we're here!" Yihwan protested. "And *oww*!"

"Oh my god. I can't believe you are all here!" Fi muttered in between gritted teeth, one hand on her hip, the other on her forehead. "What the fuck have you done? How did you even—oh my god, did you *lie* to me, Jo Yihwan? All that fuss about Justin wanting to discuss something?"

"Noona, aren't you happy to see us?" Minchan asked. Steven did the same, but with his infuriating puppy eyes. The fact that he was wearing a *Save a Drum, Bang a Drummer* shirt made his appeal seem somewhat tainted.

Yihwan felt a little sorry seeing Fi this rattled, perhaps thinking of all the possible repercussions of their actions.

"Keurae, jal deureo." Her index finger was raised now, and they knew better than to talk when that happened. "Minchan, I'm really very happy to see you, but...*dear God in heaven*. We are all going to be in very deep shit if, god forbid, something bad happens to any of you. Go back to the hotel now." She snapped her fingers twice. "Jigeum dangjang! What if the staff look for you?"

Steven's grin was confident when he said "Got that taken care of."

"And the fans? How did you—"

The magnae smiled. "Got that taken care of, too."

Yihwan stepped forward and put his hands on her shoulders. "Relax. We'll go back to the hotel as scheduled, and no one will even notice we're gone. Except for those who already know."

He noticed the scratch on her face and instinctively brought a hand up to her cheek, but Fi stepped back.

"You guys are going to be the death of me, jinjja."

Steven called for a group hug, and they ended up a messy pile of limbs and laughter on the floor.

"No way. *No way!*" Fi exclaimed, laughing, as Minchan showed her the series of Instagram and KakaoStory photos he took in the hotel.

In one of the photos, Steven and Yihwan were having a meal together. One had Yihwan studying some set pieces by the window. And then there was Steven playing a game on his phone while seated near a digital alarm clock they've tampered with to show a later time.

"And there's lots more for backup on Yihwan hyung and Steven hyung's phones," he said, explaining their strategy of being fanservice-y to keep the fans preoccupied.

"We left the hotel at a little past three." Minchan opened his Instagram account and showed Fi. "I posted the first photo thirty minutes later, while we were riding a tricycle to get here."

Said photo was a selfie of Minchan with Yihwan napping in the background. (Caption: Hyung, wake up. We still have a lot of things to do!)

It had 3,000+ likes and 200+ comments so far.

"Wait, *what*? You rode a tricycle?"

The bassist nodded. "We meant to ride the cab all the way here but the driver said something about the streets being too narrow and probably flooded."

"So we got off, took a tricycle, and a styroboat," Steven narrated. "It was fun!"

Fi could only stare at them, slack-jawed. "Did you even realize how dangerous that was?"

"Aw, come on... where's your sense of adventure?" Steven quipped. "Do you remember when we got lost at the Umeda Station in Osaka?"

"Or when we lost genius over here in The Forbidden City?" Yihwan added, jerking his thumb toward Steven. The drummer proudly grinned. "Fun times."

Fi only smiled at the recollection, then chuckled at the mental image of EG Project getting scrunched into a small jeepney just like Gabriel had been the day before. As the boys continued narrating (and exaggerating) the lengths they went through to get here, Fi allowed herself to relax and enjoy a hot cup of coffee with them. Never mind that they've all gathered inside her room; they've been held in smaller dressing rooms, after all.

"So..." she began, taking a sip off her cup. "Do you have any idea how things are going back in Seoul?"

The boys exchanged glances, but none of them seemed eager to volunteer any information. Gabriel had advised her to stay away from the internet for now, but Fi was also dying to know what was going on.

They heard a knock just as Yihwan was about to speak. Steven, who was seated in Fi's old computer chair, slid the seat over and opened the door.

It was Gabriel, and he looked more than a little upset.

Excerpt post from OrigiNation, the Official Message Board of EG Project's Fan Club
Subject | WHO IS THIS BITCH?

:kyungmi<3yihwan
(Embedded in post: Various pictures of Fi in different locations, captured in fan photos in airports, malls, backstage shots, and old photos posted by the band members themselves. They are all labeled with date, location, and other information available.)

This is Filipina Legaspi from the Philippines. She has been working with our boys since their debut. I think she is some type of coordi or road manager or something. You can see she's already part of their staff during their first few fan meets and gigs.

An Original unni who is friends with someone working in Amethyst said she used to date Steven Bae during the Sophomore Year era. They were often found spending time by themselves at Amethyst's rehearsal room when Yihwan and Minchan weren't around. There are also rumors that she got into Amethyst because she is in some kind of relationship with one of the big bosses. Disgusting.

She obviously knows how to manipulate people, and she probably did the same to Yihwan. Just thinking about her and Yihwan together makes me want to vomit. And if it's really true that she dated Steven before, how dare she seduce Yihwan too? And is Minchan her next victim?

:originamjunghwa
I do recognize her from all the EGP fan signings I've been to for the past four years! I'd kill to have a job like hers because she looks so

close to the boys. Turns out she's closer to them than we think, if you know what I mean.

:yiven5ever
Me too, I recognize her! She received a gift for Yihwan before at the airport because the band wasn't allowed to reach through the railings. Back then, I thought it was so nice of her. Now I don't know what to think anymore.

:minchan0229
She had better not touch Minchan or she will die.

:originkangjiseon
Guys, a Thai fan reported that this woman was attacked by an Original at the airport in BKK. Mad props to that fan, but if it were me, I'd have crippled that bitch.

TRACK NINE
Toe the Line

THE WALL SEPARATING FI'S ROOM from her elder sister's—the one where Gabriel and Yihwan were having a heated argument—was made of plywood, and there was no need to put one's ear against the wall to be privy to the conversation. That was how Fi started listening to KPop all those years ago, after all. Mayumi Legaspi blasted music in her room whenever she'd come home from university, and Fi heard it in all its catchy yet incomprehensible glory.

"I'm sure you've already heard about the developments back in Seoul. Stocks have crashed, and the big boss is furious. We're trying our best to divert the people's attention to Silverazzi's comeback and Steven receiving a drama offer, but the fans are relentless. There is really nothing else we could do at this point but to wait for the issue to die a natural death..."

"Really? That's the best you can do?"

"Then what more do you expect from us, Yihwan? Shut the internet down with our bare hands?"

"Oh, that's really clever. Why don't you do *that?*"

With a glance at Steven and Minchan, Fi knew both boys were tuned in to the conversation despite attempting not to look so blatant about it. Steven had been staring at that magazine page for the longest time now, and Minchan was just absentmindedly nibbling on a piece of pan de sal. It was almost like the kids had been shoved into this room because a hostile marital discussion was going on in the next.

"Look, Jo Yihwan-ssi." Gabriel's diplomatic tone turned stern, Fi noticed it in the way he addressed the band leader formally.

"My team is doing the best we can to cover all this up, all right? Just these past two days, we've had to come up with *crap* to shove down people's throats. But why aren't they buying any of it?

Because sometimes people are just waiting for an opportunity to see a good man go down. Like it or not, *this* is the opportunity some people have been waiting for. For the perfect band leader to crash and burn.

"And what you did today does not, in any way, help the situation. It's stupid and reckless. You could have gotten yourselves in trouble."

Both were silent for a few beats until Gabriel spoke again. "You're lucky, Yihwan-ssi. Fans might throw stones at you now for *allegedly* sleeping with a woman, but one hit song is enough for them to forget that. But Fi? She isn't a celebrity who can turn things around with some cheap publicity stunt, and people will always remember her as—and excuse my language, but this is verbatim, posted on EG Project's message board—*the whore who had the gall to sleep with Jo Yihwan.*"

The only other sound they heard after that was of the door being banged shut.

For the first time in years, the Legaspi dining table was completely occupied by more people than books or paperwork, and Diana couldn't hide her enthusiasm. She wouldn't stop apologizing for serving a "mediocre" set of dishes, though.

"Please don't worry about it," Gabriel said with a reassuring smile. "We were the ones who imposed..." He threw a glance at Yihwan, and his expression shifted to a more severe one, albeit fleetingly.

Fi could only shake her head. That her mother's definition of "mediocre" meant pork sinigang, stove-grilled tilapia, salted egg and green mango salad, and leche flan meant she had recently updated her dictionary. In this household, this much food was a feast.

The dining table was a medium-sized six-seater, and Fi realized how peculiar the seating arrangement was when she finally took a seat. During Gabriel's first meal here, Diana insisted he take the kabisera because he was a guest. Now that the trio was here as well, Yihwan naturally gravitated toward the opposite end of the table. On the band leader's left sat Fi, then Diana, and Steven and Minchan sat on his right.

Fi didn't think the two alpha males should be staring each other down during dinner, especially when they've just gotten out of a verbal argument, but it wasn't like she could do anything about it.

"Please, enjoy your meal," Diana finally said after saying grace, and Minchan excitedly dug into the bowl of sinigang. He had his eyes on the dish the moment he was told it was a near equivalent of his favorite tom yum goong.

"Yihwan-ah." Fi snapped her fingers in front of him, bringing his attention back to the present.

"Yeah?"

"I was asking if you wanted soup." She gently nudged a small bowl of sinigang toward him.

The band leader nodded, took the bowl, and thanked her. Yihwan ate in silence, complimenting Diana a little later after tasting every dish on the table. "Food's good," he simply said, loud enough to get Steven to agree. Minchan already expressed his opinion by helping himself to a second serving.

The loud buzzing of Yihwan's phone against the table interrupted their small talk, and Fi caught a glimpse of Haera's avatar when it popped up on the screen.

Yihwan grabbed his phone and excused himself from the table.

"Heard the weather is bad out there and thought to call."

No kidding, Yihwan thought. He could barely make out Haera's voice through the sound of hard rain hitting tin roofs. They really might have to stay for the night.

"Yihwan-ah."

Once, a long time ago, the very same voice uttering his name would have sent butterflies fluttering in Jo Yihwan's stomach. Hearing Haera's voice on the phone had been a nightly ritual for them, and listening to her tell him about her day, laugh at his jokes, or sigh over a new song he had written used to bring him so much joy.

Haera's voice used to be the melody his heart danced to.

"We're fine."

"That's good. How are the boys doing?"

Yihwan pinched the bridge of his nose. "I'm sorry. I was under the impression that we are two people who shouldn't be having this kind of conversation."

"You answered my call."

"I was being polite."

There was silence on the other line, and Yihwan knew he had hit a nerve. He didn't really care. He might still have feelings for Haera, but if he so much as caved in to her charms again...

"I miss you, Yihwan. I really do," she confessed. He tried his hardest to ignore the crack in her voice as she spoke. "I feel like shit for doing that to you. It's just that there were a lot of things to consider, a lot that could fall apart. I panicked."

Yihwan understood aftermaths very well, especially for someone like Han Haera, whose name alone assured billions of won in sales. One wrong move, and she could lose everything in the blink of an eye.

Gabriel's words echoed in his head: *Sometimes people are just waiting for an opportunity to see a good man go down*. Even after everything Haera had put him through, Yihwan would never wish for her downfall.

"Yihwan, won't you forgive me?"

The hand pressed on his forehead travelled all the way to the nape of his neck, squeezing hard, as though a little pressure would help him think clearly. Forgiveness was easy when the heart has healed, and Yihwan knew he was nowhere near that yet.

"Not yet, noona."

"I'll wait."

"It's funny," Yihwan said, swallowing the lump in his throat with much effort. "Do you remember how I said the very same words to you when you were breaking up with me? Do you remember what you told me?"

Haera didn't reply.

"You told me not to."

Steven's voice was bouncing off the dining room walls when Yihwan returned much later. The drummer made everyone at the table laugh over a cautionary tale that involved stage pyrotechnics and a bad cold, and Yihwan lingered a few strides away, down the hall where he could clearly see a laughing, happy Fi Legaspi.

He needed a few more seconds to get his head on straight, pull his emotions down a peg or two.

"Seeing you getting sprayed with a fire extinguisher was the highlight of that concert!" Minchan exclaimed, chuckling. Even Gabriel seemed to have forgotten the incidents of the past hour as he laughed along with everyone.

As Steven introduced another concert mishap story (this time involving drumsticks and a cameraman), Yihwan caught sight of Fi leaving her seat. She headed over to where he stood, hand reaching for his arm.

"Kwaenchanha?" she asked, her voice almost inaudible.

He only looked at her and didn't say a word. Her eyes were as warm as they've always been, but those same eyes now singed him for some reason. Still, he wanted more of that warmth, but thought it wrong to want more of her when all he could offer was the mess that he was, when he knew he was only looking for an anchor to keep him from drifting away.

"Yihwan-ah."

Her voice sounded different now, too, for some reason he couldn't explain. Nothing in its inflection had changed, and there was no trace of agenda in the way she uttered his name other than to let him know she was there, willing to listen to whatever he needed to say. But now it made him feel something else; like she was crushing his heart in her hand every time his name escaped her lips.

Listlessly, Yihwan stepped forward, and Fi closed the gap between them. A second later, he was holding her in his arms and she was running a hand up and down his back. Encouraging. Reassuring. Not a word had left his mouth, and yet here she was, so ready to provide the comfort he needed.

He closed his eyes on instinct, for a while just grateful for her.

To: Gabriel Park <gabrielpark@amethystent.com>
From: Jillian Montinola <jmontinola@jumpproductions.com>
Date: August 07, 10:53 p.m.
Subject: EG Project Leap of Faith MNL

Dear Mr. Park,

As discussed briefly over the phone before our reception got unbearably choppy, we at Jump Productions are recommending that EG Project's Leap of Faith concerts be cancelled in light of Typhoon Choleng, which might be staying in the country for at least two more days. Since we are holding the concert in an outdoor venue, we are concerned over the safety of your band, staff, our crew, as well as the fans attending. There is no way we can push through with this concert under these weather conditions.

We are willing, however, to rebook EG Project for another date. Kindly give us at least a month to secure a venue. Of course, this is also up to the band's schedule. We understand that their schedules are packed.

Please let me know Amethyst's decision on this matter. As regards matters of finance, kindly expect a call from our agency within the next 24 hours. We are very sorry for the inconvenience.

Jillian Montinola
Event Organizer, Jump Productions PH

...

To: Jillian Montinola <jmontinola@jumpproductions.com>
From: Gabriel Park <gabrielpark@amethystent.com>

Date: August 08 at 2:12 a.m.
Subject: RE: EG Project Leap of Faith MNL

Dear Ms. Montinola,

Amethyst Entertainment has been informed of and understands the situation at hand. Although we are saddened that both parties' efforts will go to waste, we accept the recommendation to cancel EG Project's scheduled concert this weekend. We are currently keeping in touch with media outlets here and in South Korea to settle matters regarding the cancellation.

Rest assured that the band will return to stage their concert in Manila, but we cannot give you a certain date as of the moment, as EG Project's schedule is booked until the end of the year.

We will be expecting your call. Thank you for your hard work.

Gabriel Park
PR Manager
Amethyst Entertainment, Seoul, South Korea

"Aren't you going to rest yet?"

Gabriel was met by Fi's curious doe eyes and a cup of coffee when he looked up from his laptop. She placed the cup on the table and sat across from him. The rain outside was now just a mild shower, but it didn't seem like it was going to stop soon.

"That's fresh, coming from *you*."

"Touché."

A smirk lined his face as he returned to his correspondence. "Are the kids asleep?"

Because the flood outside hadn't yet subsided, the band decided to stay at Fi's house for the night. Gabriel wasn't exactly thrilled by the idea, but the band's safety was their priority. Phone calls were made to the entourage to keep them in the loop, and the band continued holding the smokescreen up, keeping their fans amused all night.

Fi laughed. In essence, that's what her job required: to "babysit" the band, manage their day-to-day activities, make sure they eat right to keep them from getting sick, make sure they observe proper decorum so as not to be branded a nuisance, and so on.

But she scrunched her nose at him too, an attempt to keep in a silly little smile over the insinuation that she and Gabriel were mom and dad. "Steven and Minchan are still on their phones, and Yihwan suddenly felt like writing something, so... no."

Gabriel lifted the cup to his lips and took a sip. "Let them be. It's the weekend, anyway."

"And the concert is cancelled."

"That, too."

"You haven't answered my question yet."

He scratched his brow and stared back at his screen. It seemed he had more e-mails to respond to, more calls to make. "Give me at least another hour."

"If you need any help..."

Gabriel raised his cup again. "This is enough. Thanks, by the way."

"You sure?"

"You should be the one getting some rest."

"Yeah... about that."

His eyes narrowed as he studied her face. "Can't sleep?"

"I heard your conversation with Yihwan before dinner," she admitted. The look on his face told her he already figured as much. "Those things that people say about me..."

"Listen, I'm sorry I even uttered those words."

"No—I... I know you were only upset over the boys' carelessness."

"Don't let them get to you."

"I'm trying my best."

Gabriel pulled his laptop screen down shut and rubbed his palms together tentatively. His lips were parted slightly, like the words he wanted to say lingered there, reluctant to slip out. "Kijoo noona's recommendation is to pull you out of EG Project's staff list for the time being. Meanwhile, you can manage Silverazzi..."

"So that's why Justin's here."

"Only until this all dies down, Fi. It shouldn't be so bad?"

She shook her head. "I've worked with Silverazzi a couple of times. Bunch of nice girls with good heads on their shoulders. I don't think there'd be a problem."

"No separation anxiety?"

"Maybe a little bit, but I'll live," she replied, laughing softly.

"Is that a yes?"

"If it's for the good of the band..."

"Filipina," Gabriel uttered her name like a sigh. "I'd really like it if you started thinking of yourself too."

And I don't know what to do with
The truth you slapped my face with
Every time I look at you now
It's like I never really knew you anyhow

I don't think I have the right to feel this
But your voice—your voice
It's tugging at my heartstrings

I reckon it beckons me
To fly to your side
But how do I
When someone's gone and clipped my wings

"This isn't right... ," Yihwan mumbled, tempted to tear the page he just filled with words to a new song.

"It really isn't."

The band leader glanced over his shoulder and saw his band mates on their phones. He sensed trouble seeing the frowns on their faces. "What is it?"

"The fans... *our* fans have tracked down Fi noona's social media accounts, and they're posting horrible things."

"These kids don't even know what they're talking about." Steven's tone was uncharacteristically stern, and Yihwan could see how hard the drummer tried to keep his cool. "How dare they put her down like this—they don't even know her!"

"We can't keep on letting them do this to her. We have to do something, hyung."

"I know." Yihwan gritted his teeth. "I just don't know *what*."

"Let's sue them," Steven suggested.

Minchan shook his head. "Do you think AmEnt is willing to shell out money for a class action lawsuit? They're already losing money over this scandal in the first place."

The two continued their debate, leaving the band leader to his thoughts. Yihwan stared at the page he had been writing on and tore it off. He used to be able to sort his issues out by writing about them, but he doubted it would be of any help now.

When Gabriel decided to wrap up, the sun was slowly peeking out in the horizon. He stretched his arms up above his head, noting the extra cup of coffee on the table in front of him. It was Fi's.

She'd kept him company until about an hour ago, when he encouraged her to go to bed after dozing off in the middle of telling him a story about her sister. She acquiesced, but reminded him to get some rest, too.

He put the cups away in the kitchen, washing them carefully and placing them on the dish rack to dry. The rain had yet to stop, but strangely enough, he had already gotten used to the sound it made over the tin roofs. It wasn't music to his ears, but he supposed he was going to associate it with Fi now, the way he did with a lot of mundane things.

She taught him the polite way to hand out business cards and give out handshakes so he wouldn't be regarded as arrogant or disrespectful. Through her, Gabriel even learned it was impolite to knock back a shot of soju—or drink *anything* for that matter—without turning away from someone who's older or of higher authority. "Your sunbae's cup must always be full, so keep pouring them drinks, but never *ever* use your left hand," he recalled her saying. "And *never* pour yourself a drink. That's rude."

He supposed it was a useless task to try pinpointing when exactly he started feeling this way for her. What he knew for certain was that she became his lifeline during his first year in Seoul, a strong rope the universe threw at him when he'd all but drowned in a culture so different from the one he grew up in. He sought her company when he felt as though everyone else looked at him like he was a fool, and she was always happy to be there for him.

At least he hoped she was.

Gabriel had adapted to the culture now. Gone were the days when his sunbae-deul would think him ill-mannered, or when his colleagues would laugh at his misinformed actions. Gone were the moments he would think twice about saying something, afraid of being misunderstood. Everything that crushed his otherwise solid self-confidence was gone, and it was mostly thanks to Fi.

But while Gabriel was thankful she was in his life, he knew it wasn't simply gratitude compelling him to shield her from a world intent on tearing her apart.

"Are you in love with her?" his mother once asked. He wasn't able to call New York a lot, especially after AmEnt changed CEOs and imposed a workaholic culture on its employees, but he did that one time. And he talked about Fi. He didn't plan it, but it happened anyway.

"I don't know."

"Hearing you talk about her makes me want to meet her."

"I wish you could. She's amazing."

Only "amazing" didn't quite cut it. Gabriel once likened Fi to a moth enticed by Jo Yihwan's flame, but that was only one way to look at the story.

The other was this:

That Fi was Gabriel's sun, and right now he needed to protect her light before it got snuffed out for good.

NEWS REPORT
Channel 8
August 8 | Manila, Philippines

[Establishing shot of Baywalk Concert Grounds, as very hard wind and rain threaten to topple over some scaffolding bearing EG Project's concert streamers]

CAPTION: South Korean pop-rock band East Genesis Project's Leap of Faith concerts cancelled due to typhoon

ELISE BONIFACIO: As the hard wind and rain from Typhoon Choleng continue to batter Metro Manila, Jump Productions, organizer and promoter of East Genesis Project's Leap of Faith concerts, has announced that they are cancelling the shows for the safety of the band and its fans.

[Video clip of Regina Jardeleza, PR head of Jump Productions]

CAPTION: Regina Jardeleza, PR Head, Jump Productions

REGINA JARDELEZA: It's been under discussion since yesterday, and since the weather really isn't getting any better, we, together with Amethyst Entertainment, have decided to cancel the shows for now. It's regrettable, yes, but we would rather cancel it now than have unfortunate incidents during the show. Since there is no new schedule for the concert yet, we will be refunding show tickets starting next week.

[Video clip of Gabriel Park, PR manager of Amethyst Entertainment]

CAPTION: Gabriel Park, PR Manager, Amethyst Entertainment

GABRIEL PARK: EG Project expresses their gratitude to the Philippine fans who have shown their support and warmth during this time. Unfortunately, the band will not be able to perform at the Baywalk Concert Grounds today and tomorrow as promised. Please be assured, however, that the band will be back for another concert, hopefully very soon!

[Video footage of Elise Bonifacio in front of the concert grounds with EG Project fans gathered behind her, wearing raincoats and holding umbrellas.]

ELISE BONIFACIO: These EG Project fans behind me have been waiting here since this morning, hoping to catch a glimpse of their idols. Sadly, they'll be going home without the concert experience they've been looking forward to for months.

Elise Bonifacio, Channel 8 News.

ABOUT FACE

"YOU KNOW...I've always worried about you"—Fi looked over her shoulder and saw her mother standing a few feet away from her, arms crossed in front of her chest—"working with those boys all the time, running yourself ragged you can't even call your mother."

Gabriel and the band had just left for the hotel in a nondescript black van, and Fi was lingering by the window where she waved them goodbye as the vehicle drove away. The rain had stopped hours ago, allowing the flood to subside and easing the traffic flow around their neighborhood.

Diana walked over, peering out the window just as the van turned at the intersection. "Filipina?"

"Ma—"

The older woman studied her daughter's face, but Fi dropped her gaze and let guilt gnaw at her heart. "I'm sorry, Ma. I'll do a better job of keeping in touch from now on."

"That doesn't sound like everything I need to hear."

Of course. There was no way her mother missed all the not-so-subtle hints of trouble. Especially not when Gabriel and Yihwan were yelling at each other the night before. Not even the language barrier could stop anyone from concluding something was amiss.

Diana only smiled, noting the reluctance in Fi's eyes when she raised her gaze to meet hers. "When did my little lady grow up like this?" she asked, raising a hand to cradle her daughter's cheek. "You used to tell your mother *everything*."

Fi blinked away the look in her eyes, the one her mother just saw, hoping she will eventually drop this conversation. She hated that she would have to lie to her mother, but it was either that or break her heart.

"I just need to sort out some things before returning to Seoul, is all."

When Diana didn't utter a word, Fi felt the need to compensate for the silence. "I'm fine, Ma."

"I believe you."

Fi exhaled the breath she'd been holding and leaned in to hug Diana. She buried her face in the crook of her mother's neck, aware of the gentle fingers that ran through her hair. The distance from this limbo she was in now to being fine was long, but Fi had already decided this was a battle she'd have to fight and win on her own. Because what good was it to tell her mother about it if it would make her feel helpless anyway?

It was Diana who pulled away first, the reassuring smile on her face still there. "Yihwan is so guwapo, ha?" she commented, the impish twinkle in her eyes reappearing. "But I think I like Gabriel more. So dashing and strong. And he seems the type to be maalaga."

"Ma."

The older woman giggled. "What—I remember you telling me about Yihwan before. He's good-looking, but he also seems like a snob."

"Ma!"

"Why, anak? You don't like him anymore? Is it because of Gabriel?"

"Maaaa!"

"All right, all right. I'll stop now." Diana laughed and pulled her daughter in for another hug. "If it were up to me, I'd never let you return to Seoul again. I've missed you so much," she said softly and dropped a kiss on Fi's hair.

There was a pause as Fi struggled to swallow the lump in her throat. "I've missed you too, Ma."

Han Haera stared at her phone as it rang. She rarely answered calls from unknown numbers, but she decided to pick up anyway.

"Yeoboseyo, Han Haera-ssi?"

"Who is this?"

"This is Fi Legaspi from AmEnt. I used to be on your entour—
"

"Fi. Wow, it's been such a long time since I last heard from you."

There was silence on the other end of the line. Haera could tell Fi was reluctant about this call, but the actress waited for her to speak. Somehow, she felt like this might be about Yihwan.

And it was. Haera fell silent when Fi asked her to stop calling Yihwan for the meantime. She hadn't noticed how her free hand clenched into a fist until Fi spoke again. "Yihwan is having a really hard time right now, and…"

"Are you implying that I have something to do with it?"

"He hasn't been himself since the rumors about you—"

"Shouldn't you be more concerned about the rumors that he's sleeping with you, Fi?"

"Haera-ssi, you know that's not true."

"No. I don't know."

"I don't care what you think about the rumors," Fi said in a huff. "And I don't want this conversation to last longer than it should. I called because I want to help Yihwan get back on his feet. Because clearly, he can't do it when you keep reminding him of what he lost."

"He wasn't the only one who lost something, Fi," Haera pointed out. "On the other hand, you will lose everything if you don't get your name cleared, and soon."

"This is not about me."

"But it should be."

Be kinder to yourself, Fi. The band is your responsibility, but you're also responsible for yourself. Don't light yourself on fire just so you can keep everyone else warm.

Fi. You stay strong through all of this, okay? Don't let the bad people mess your head up.

Well, that was unexpected.

Haera's sentiments echoed Gabriel's in a way, but the actress' sincerity surprised her. Ever since Haera broke up with Yihwan, Fi had filed her name under the category "Selfish, Heartless Bitches."

How wrong of her to slap that label on Haera, when she only knew Yihwan's side of the story. How did that make her any better than the sasaengs who called her names on the Internet?

Mianhaeyo, Haera-ssi.

As she mulled over the actress's words, she recalled the offer Gabriel mentioned. Nothing's been set in stone, but AmEnt seemed to think it necessary. She remembered Gabriel telling her to think of herself too, making her wonder if it was so wrong to have spent all her time and effort on her band.

The opening notes of *Stuff of Daydreams* pulled her out of her reverie. Gabriel was calling.

"Please tell me you've arrived safe and sound."

"Yes," he replied. "Yes, we have. I'm sorry this call is late. Lots of stuff going on."

"Nah, it's fine. I was worried your van was followed or something. My view from the window wasn't exactly the best..."

"Oh, but I like that window. Lots of history." Gabriel's laughter sounded warm over the phone; it was as though he was just standing next to her. The thought made her smile.

"Uh-oh. What did you hear from Mom?"

He laughed some more. "Incriminating things."

"Planning to blackmail me?"

"O-ho. Blackmail material about you *exists*?" He was about to say something more, but his other phone started to ring. "Sorry, Fi...can I put you on hold for a bit? I'll just take this call."

"Sure, go ahead," she said, entertaining herself by walking into Mayumi's room and looking through her old stuff.

She stumbled upon a box, a collection of CDs rescued from the first flood that almost destroyed their house years back. Most of

78

the CD covers have been painstakingly restored, but she could still see the extent of the water damage. Mold clung to the acrylic casings, and Fi reminded herself to try and clean them up the next day.

"Still there, Fi?"

"Yeah."

"You were very quiet."

"I was just looking through some of my unni's old collections." She was holding a g.o.d. *Chapter 4* album, one of the many memorabilia that the flood completely damaged. "Gabe, do you know g.o.d.?"

"I know of them, but I don't know them personally."

"Do you know the song *Road*?"

"I'm not sure I've heard it. Why?"

"Nothing, I just... thought of it. I'm holding my unni's old g.o.d. album that has the song."

"Why don't you play it for me?" he asked. She could hear paper shuffling in the background; he was probably staying up late again to finish some more work. Meanwhile, here she was, restless and looking for something to do.

"Can't. Most of these ones I'm looking at right now were damaged by a flood many years back," Fi said, regretful. "The ones on the shelves you saw were the newer ones. Maybe when I return to Seoul, I'll look for replacements for these and surprise my unni when she returns from... wherever."

"Bummer. Is it a good song?"

"Got me into KPop."

"Reason enough for me to look it up."

She smiled and reminded him to keep his priorities in check. "I'll go monitor the weather for the meantime."

"All right. No peeking anywhere else, Ms. Legaspi."

"Heard you loud and clear, Mr. Park. Good night."

Fi let the call linger long enough for her to hear him chuckle and say "Good night." But instead of checking the weather forecast like she said she would, she found herself lying on her sister's bed. Without the boys around, the house was silent again, and she relished that, if only for the fact that she was able to gather her thoughts.

There were times in the past—even after Mayumi left to work overseas—when she'd sought the comfort of this room whenever something troubled her. Simply being in this room reminded her of the heart-to-heart talks she and Mayumi had all those years, all the secrets shared between them, as well as the tears.

It still did.

But as she shifted to lie on her side, she caught a whiff of Gabriel's cologne on the sheets and pillows. Slowly, she curled up against one of the pillows and closed her eyes.

Eight hours later, she woke up from a peaceful, dreamless sleep.

FROM FI LEGASPI'S KAKAOSTORY FEED

Filipina Legaspi
11 months ago (103 hearts, 1,823 comments)

Exhausted.

-With Yihwan, Steven, and Minchan
(Photo attachment: All four of them sitting on EG Project's couch—
from left to right: Yihwan, Fi, Steven, and Minchan—pretending to
be asleep. From the angle, it seems Minchan took the photo with
his arm outstretched, but it's barely noticeable.)

COMMENTS

We should have known this picture meant something else entirely.
Garbage.

God, please don't let it be true that she has infected the magnae
too. Yihwan, Steven—we'll forgive you if you drop that slut out of
your entourage.

If you have a shred of dignity left in you, just leave.

Oh look, an actual pic of them after a foursome.

I'm so embarrassed to be a FilOriginal because of her.

I used to think this photo was so cute and heartwarming. Now it
disgusts me.

I hope for your sake that the sex was good, because that's going to be
your last.

TRACK ELEVEN

UNRAVELS

"**M**INCHAN, I NEED A HAND PLEASE!" Steven called from the bedroom while cramming the rest of his clothes and some fan gifts into his suitcase.

"I'm busy!"

The drummer cursed under his breath. *Eish, jinjja.* Minchan could be such a little shit sometimes.

"Ya! Daeche mweoya?" he asked, annoyed. The bassist had been glued to his tablet all night, and Steven figured he wasn't just playing games or binge-watching movies. Steven walked out to their suite's common area and found Minchan sitting on the carpet, writing something on his small notebook. His tablet, propped up against a cup of coffee, was playing a YouTube video.

Minchan didn't even bother looking up when he mumbled, "Research." Steven caught the words "Sticks and stones may break my bones, but words can hurt me too" from the video before looking over Minchan's shoulder.

"New song?"

"Possibly."

The longer Steven stared at the words Minchan scribbled on his notebook, the clearer his intent became. Steven sat with him. "Melody?"

"No progress on that yet."

In no time, Steven began tapping his fingers on the table, humming a tune. Minchan caught on and transposed some of the words he wrote, working within the melody his hyung just came up with.

"I think we may have something here, Chan-ah."

Steven pulled the notebook toward him when Minchan put his pen down and let the words linger in his brain a bit. He grinned. It had the makings of a really good song.

"Jal haesseo, Minchan-ah!" Steven said, beaming at their magnae with pride.

Minchan's eyes lit up. "You really think so?"

"Yep!" Steven smacked Minchan's back, got up and took the notebook hostage as he walked back into the bedroom. "We'll finish up later. Now help me pack."

On a regular day, it was easy for Yihwan to pass out in the airplane within ten minutes of getting settled into his seat. Long flight or not, he took every opportunity to catch up on sleep.

Today was an exception, and it's that damn PR hotshot's fault Yihwan couldn't keep still.

It was as if someone set a fire somewhere in his chest when Justin told them today that Fi was flying back to Seoul the next morning with Gabriel. He'd clenched his fists inside his pockets when he confirmed this with the PR guy.

"I heard you're staying behind with Fi. Does it have to be you?"

"Did you want it to be you?"

"As a matter of fact, I did. She's still part of the band's entourage, and—"

"No. As of five days ago, she isn't part of EG Project's entourage anymore."

Gabriel went on to say this was for Fi's best interests, noting the airport incident in Thailand, and the continuous rumor-mongering among the Originals. Yihwan thought otherwise.

"Do you like her?"

"I don't think that's any of your business, Yihwan-ssi. But if you must know—yes, I do like her. Is there a problem?"

Yihwan shut his eyes tight. *Yes, there is a problem*, he thought, succumbing to a truth he was still struggling to come to terms with. *This is unacceptable.*

It was obviously an ice cream cone, what Fi has just handed to him. But it looked so ridiculously tiny in his hand that Gabriel felt like she was pulling some kind of prank on him.

"It's ice cream, Gabe. *Dirty* ice cream." She started enjoying her cone before he could react to what it's called.

She chuckled and sat beside him on the ledge facing the bay. The weather was much kinder today, allowing them a majestic view of the sunset. Around them, people went about their lives—vendors worked hard selling various wares, students milled about while enjoying street food, couples strolled leisurely while holding hands—all of them unaware, uncaring of the heavy weight Fi carried in her heart.

It was their last day in Manila. Tomorrow, she would have to face the mess she unwittingly made. Tomorrow, she would have to make decisions she still wasn't sure would be good for everyone.

"Why would you feed me something dirty?"

She looked at Gabriel and managed a smile. "It's just what people call it because it's ice cream being sold on the streets. You know, pollution and all." Truthfully, Fi didn't really know if that was an accurate interpretation of the moniker, but Gabriel seemed sold. He took another look at the purple, yellow, and brown lumps piled on top of the sugar cone before finally tasting it.

"Mmm. Is there cheese in this?"

"Yep. Yellow one's cheese. Purple is ube, and the brown one's chocolate."

"Oh, I like the cheese."

"Oh, I *know*," she said, meaning something else entirely. The way Gabriel laughed told her the reference wasn't lost on him.

They fell silent after that, enchanted by the slow setting sun in the distance. A magnificent mix of orange, yellow, and purple hues filled the sky until dusk settled in and snatched the day away.

"I wish I could be a sunset," she said, and Gabriel turned his head just in time to see her wipe away tears. "No one ever looks at a sunset and feels disgusted. People always think it's so beautiful and magical...and this is something they could see every day. It's not a miracle or a rare phenomenon like an eclipse. Or a meteor shower. But still..."

"Still... they find beauty in an everyday occurrence?"

"Yeah."

"How do you know you're *not* a sunset?"

Her expression was incredulous when Fi looked at him. "I'm not. I'm... dirty ice cream."

Gabriel glanced at his sugar cone. "Well, you *are* sweet, I'll give you that."

"People say I'm dirty."

The smile on his face faded. "I told you not to look—"

"I know. I told myself I could take it," she said. "I didn't do anything wrong. I was just doing my job. Why should I be afraid of these people calling me names?"

More tears fell. "But then I realized I wasn't so strong, after all."

"Fi..."

"The offer for reassignment still stands, right?" Fi carelessly wiped her face and tried to compose herself.

"Yes."

"How soon can I take it?"

"Are you sure you want to do this?"

"I love my band, Gabe. If the fans want to ruin me, they can do that without dragging EG Project into this."

The band had so much more to lose; that was how Fi saw it. The pettiness of it all irked her, but she knew this was how the entertainment industry worked. Once an idol's image got tainted, it wouldn't take long until everything they've worked for came crashing down like a house of cards.

She would never allow that.

"But I want to keep my job too," she candidly admitted. "I've grown to love what I do, and I want to keep doing it. I want to be there when these talented people I work with touch people's hearts and minds with their craft. I want to be backstage, clapping their shoulders and hugging them for a job well done. I want to encourage them to continue being who they are, to not lose themselves to the spotlight..."

"You do that well," Gabriel said. He chucked his sugar cone into a nearby trash bin and shifted on the ledge to face her. Slowly and with care, his hands reached for the strands of her hair, fingers tucking them behind her ears.

Maybe it was because she's been crying and the tears have cleared her vision that Fi was taken aback when she realized Gabriel's face was *thisclose* to hers.

So close, she could almost map out constellations with the freckles on his face.

So close her heart almost came to a halt just looking into his brown eyes, which seemed to be searching through hers.

His perfectly carved lips were moving now, but there was at least a five-millisecond discrepancy between him uttering words and her actually being able to hear them.

"And I want to tell you not to lose yourself in this mess."

"I won't," Fi said simply, averting her gaze. The smell of his cologne reminded her of the pillow she held close as she slept the night before. The mere image of Gabriel in place of that pillow made her heart race.

No, Fi. This is Yihwan redux, she thought and turned away, knowing she'd be in trouble once again if she didn't nip this— whatever this was—in the bud.

[BREAKING NEWS] Han Haera and Jung Hwichan Have Broken Up
August 12 | Dispatch

At the launch of her new film, *Yeouido Afternoon*, top actress Han Haera surprised everyone after addressing persistent rumors about her relationship with fellow actor Jung Hwichan.

"Jung Hwichan and I have gone our separate ways. We are thankful to everyone who supported our relationship as well as our individual careers, but I guess it's true what they say: Some good things never really last."

The actress did not offer any reason or explanation for the break up.

Very recently, the actress had been caught up in dating rumors involving East Genesis Project's band leader, Jo Yihwan, but these were quickly denied by their agencies.

It remains to be seen how this news will affect Han Haera's film, which will be hitting theaters in less than a month.

COMMENTS

[+6,521, -4,091] Okay, now tell us: Which politician embezzled money?

[+5,902, -3,322] I really think there's something between her and Jo Yihwan. The die-hard sasaengs can try their best to defend him, but there are eyewitness accounts saying Yihwan was always drunk after the dating rumors were denied. Let's not even get started on that hotel scandal with the staff member. And to think Yihwan is one of the more respectable guys in the industry. Man's a mess now.

[+3,001, -1,720] My heart is breaking. I was rooting for Hwira couple all the way!

[+2,056, -864] Choigo Entertainment's stocks are dropping thanks to you, Han Haera.

[+1,465, -784] Getting back with Jo Yihwan in 3, 2...

TRACK TWELVE
HERO/ZERO

S EOUL FELT EVEN MORE CHAOTIC than it was when they left it. At least that's how it seemed to Yihwan hours after they arrived. While EG Project was on a plane back to Korea, Han Haera had announced her breakup with Jung Hwichan, prompting netizens to connect disjointed puzzle pieces and jump to conclusions.

I told you they were dating! They've probably gotten smarter about keeping their relationship under wraps, but they totally are still together!

Han Haera is a two-timing bitch. And Jo Yihwan isn't any better, either.

Jo Yihwan and Han Haera. One is desperate to bed someone and the other is a cheater. You deserve each other.

Phone pressed to his ear, Yihwan skimmed through netizen comments on his tablet. From the corner of his eye, he spied Steven and Minchan throwing him wary looks and whispering to each other. He wouldn't put it past them to be placing bets on who he was calling or what other blunder he would manage to get himself into, but he was in no mood to play along. He shot them both a glare, and they exited the room together.

It took a long time before his call was answered.

"Yeobose—"

"Mwohaneungeoya jigeum?"

"Welcome back."

"Answer me, noona. What the fuck are you doing?"

"I broke up with Hwichan. People do that sometimes..."

"Explain to me how you are still so calm about this. Did you plan this to hurt me even more?"

When Haera uttered his name, it was as though her hands have reached out to him, holding his face and willing him to look at her. To stay still and listen. "We've already broken up, Yihwan. I think it'll help if we both acknowledged that," she told him calmly, like she had rehearsed this all along while waiting for his call. "Should everything be about you?"

"My name is *everywhere* in this, if you haven't noticed." He knew he should at least try to act calmer than this, but Haera's utter lack of consideration infuriated him so. "I haven't even recovered from—"

"Are you still breathing?"

"What?"

"You're still breathing."

"What does that have to do with anyth—"

"This won't kill you. The difference between you and me and someone else who doesn't live under the limelight like us is that we can lose as much as we have gained and just get back up. We have money. Machinery. Influence. There are people behind us pulling strings and keeping the skeletons in our closet. This is *nothing* to us."

Yihwan shook his head. "What are you even talking about?"

"Yihwan, how long do you think Fi will survive…getting bashed and called names all over these websites?"

A pause. "You…did this for Fi?"

"Don't act so surprised," Haera said, her voice sounding like she was smiling. "I only threw bait."

Yihwan hated it when he doesn't get what he wants. He wasn't a brat per se, but he worked hard for the things he wanted, and he knew when he should be getting something he deserved.

There were things, however, that even hard workers couldn't control.

He didn't mind the screaming fans outside the Amethyst Entertainment building yelling curses at him, didn't worry when they were told so early in the morning that the company's stocks were dropping by the hour because he was involved in yet another "scandal." He minded that it was Justin who broke the news. He minded that it was Justin—not Fi—who came to the dorm and fetched them for the day's scheduled appointments.

His fists were clenched as he stormed through the seventh floor corridors, agitated over Justin's words echoing in his head.

Didn't Fi tell you? She'd been reassigned to Silverazzi for the meantime.

This has got to be some kind of joke. Though Fi was by no means exclusively tied to EG Project, it was a sort of unwritten, unspoken rule. Four years of working together built an undeniable bond among them, making the band members fiercely possessive of their favorite girl Friday.

Which explained why Yihwan now felt confused. And angry.

There was a piece of paper with the name Silverazzi scrawled on it taped to the door of the Topaz rehearsal room, and the band leader stared at the name for a good three seconds before twisting the knob open. His knocking came right after.

"Sunbae!" The collective greeting came from a group of five young ladies sitting on the wooden floor at the far end of the room. They all stood up and bowed to Yihwan, who mustered a sincere smile and returned the gesture. His gaze, however, was fixed on the sixth lady who had been sitting with the Silverazzi members when he came in.

"May I borrow Fi for a minute?" he asked.

Fi responded quickly, "We're in the middle of a schedule alignment..."

"Just a minute. Please."

The Silverazzi ladies looked at Fi, then Yihwan, and Fi once again. The road manager closed her scheduler and excused herself. "Kkatda olkke."

"Ne, sunbaenim!"

As soon as the door was shut behind her, Yihwan's hand clamped over her wrist in a death grip. Fi was speechless as he pulled her toward the stairwell. She'd seen this in K-dramas many times before, but she always thought this rather brusque gesture belonged to those fictional universes. Not in real life.

Not in *her* life.

"You got reassigned. To Silverazzi," were Yihwan's first words when they finally reached the stairwell. His voice bounced against the walls, and Fi was starting to think this was a bad place to have this conversation.

Fi stared at him, unsure if he had anything else to say. It surprised her how intimidated she was by the way he hovered over her. She had never felt this way before. Then again, Yihwan was agitated and frustrated, and all of this negative energy was directed at her.

"... and your question is?"

"Why?"

For a full five seconds, she thought of casually citing the non-exclusivity clauses in her job description, but Fi couldn't find it in her to shoot him down like that. This shouldn't be a hostile conversation, even if she felt Yihwan was close to throwing a punch.

"You know *exactly* why."

"No. I don't. I can't understand why you would suddenly give up on us just like that."

"You really think I gave up on you?"

"Yes."

Fi's eyes started to sting, and she was certain she was going to break down if she so much as uttered a word. If she stayed with the band, things were just going to get worse. Merely getting photographed with them now was gossip fodder, fuel to the hate. How many more terrible insults would be thrown at them, then? Enough perhaps to bury the band and everything they've worked for all these years.

She steeled herself, looked him in the eye. "If you can't understand why I'm doing this, then maybe you don't know me at all." Fi shook his hand off her wrist and turned away, but two strides later, he was already blocking the door.

"Fi... you don't understand. I *need* you."

If this happened a year or so ago, those words would be enough to make her knees wobble. But now, even as her heart raced, she didn't feel anything else. It wasn't that Yihwan's words sounded empty. In fact, she believed he was as sincere as ever.

Now, Fi felt nothing else but a dull ache in her chest that reminded her of how much she used to love him.

"There's just this..." And there it was, that all too familiar look in Yihwan's eyes when he began to lose his grasp on words and turn into an imbecile. When he brought a hand to his chest, Fi couldn't help but feel like he lodged a knife in her gut. "I keep thinking about you, Fi. Since that night in Bangkok... I realized what an idiot I've been, not being able to see something precious that's right beside me."

No, Yihwan. Don't.

"And the more I don't see you, the more I feel scared I'm going to lose you."

Damn it. Don't do this.

She knew where this conversation was headed, and she wanted none of it. "Talk to me when you're done being emotional about this," she said and hurried down to the sixth floor instead.

He chased after her and cornered her on the landing. "Fi, please... just listen to me."

Yihwan was panting now, his chest visibly heaving under the gray V-neck he was wearing. "I think I'm in love with you, Fi. I can't find any other reason why I'm feeling this way..."

Now her knees trembled, but she couldn't seem to place her emotions. Should she be happy hearing this? Regretful? Cynical? Surely Yihwan was being irrational, uttering a word almost synonymous to the name Han Haera.

"You're not in love with me, Yihwan-ah. You're in love with the *idea* of being in love with someone."

"No, you don't understand!" he insisted, mouth hanging open, unable to say anything else. Suddenly, she felt sorry for the typically eloquent Jo Yihwan who couldn't express himself with

93

his weapon of choice. "You…you're all I could think of. You're like…you're this persistent refrain I can't get out of my head no matter wh—"

"See *that's* the thing. I never wanted to be a refrain in your head." Her voice was laced with conviction as she spoke, but she was blinking away tears.

"I wanted to be the song."

The band leader stood there agape, defeated, and with nothing else to say. He was motionless until Fi turned around to leave. Three seconds tops, and Yihwan's lips were on hers, forceful and awkward.

A loud smack echoed throughout the stairwell.

Fact: Gossip travels faster than the speed of light.

Or South Korea's LTE speed. Or your coworkers' running mouths. Whichever applies.

Coworkers' running mouths it is, Fi decided, as she sat opposite the interim CEO's executive assistant, Jin Sangwook. Mr. Jin eyed her rather severely, and she braced herself for a scolding. She expected him to recite something off the AmEnt employee manual, something about work ethics and morals and getting involved with talents. He would probably remind her that she was still in hot water for the Bangkok incident, too.

Instead, Mr. Jin engaged in a phone call for the next several minutes. Fi gathered nothing from the man's curt utterances of "yes," "no," and "I understand," and she was compelled to ask if they should postpone this discussion to another day. But the phone call ended just then, and Mr. Jin pulled out a brown envelope from his suitcase.

"Ms. Legaspi, I was instructed to give you this." He slid the brown envelope toward her. She looked at him curiously, and he simply gestured for her to open it. Her head spun when she obliged and saw the document header.

Contract Termination.

Song Minchan Is a Bully, Part 1
Uploaded on EG Project's Youtube Channel
TRT: 1min 45secs

[Disclaimer on screen, white over black:

No Baes were harmed in the making of this film.
Okay, maybe just a little bit.
In the feels.]

0:05   [CAPTION: EG Project dressing room]
Steven enters the room with a cup of coffee and a box of
doughnuts. He sits on the couch and waits. Minchan comes in. He
sits beside Steven and opens the box of doughnuts, even when
Steven clearly says no. Laughing, Minchan just casually grabs the
whole box and runs away.

0:23   [CAPTION: EG Project music space]
The band is at rehearsal, and Yihwan calls for a break. When
Steven leaves the room for a bit, Minchan hides Steven's
drumsticks away without Yihwan noticing. Later, they resume
rehearsal, but Steven looks confused because he couldn't find his
drumsticks. Yihwan tells him he must be turning senile while
Minchan cackles in his spot.

0:49   [CAPTION: EG Project van]
Minchan shows the camera a piece of tissue he just rolled into a
thin stick. He then points the camera at Steven, who is sleeping
soundly beside him, and proceeds to stick the pointy end of the
tissue into the drummer's nose. Steven sneezes.

1:16   [CAPTION: Amethyst Entertainment conference room]
Minchan, while looking over promotional photos: Is it just me or
does Steven hyung look ugliest of us three?
(Steven protests by snatching the photo away from him. Yihwan
laughs.)
Minchan: I seriously don't know how you got so many fans.

COMMENTS

"At first I found it funny, and then I got increasingly annoyed for Steven. I'm not even a fan."

"Minchan, you're still the magnae, remember that. Have some respect."

"The fact that Yihwan just laughs at Minchan's rudeness at 1:32 makes me sick."

"Poor *Baeby*. How is Minchan allowed to treat a hyung like this?"

"This just proves all the EG Project stories about Minchan being a brat. You can't say the boys are just having fun. Steven looked so annoyed when Minchan woke him up in the van."

TRACK THIRTEEN
TU ME MANQUES

F I WOKE UP DISORIENTED THE NEXT DAY, cursing when she stubbed her big toe against the foot of the bedside table. For the first time in years, she'd actually overslept.

She grumbled all the way to the bathroom, checking her phone for messages. She was willing to bet the 15 missed calls and 23 unread messages were from Yihwan alone.

Her eyes felt like they were burning, but they looked even worse. *This is what you get for crying all night, Fi*, she told herself, pausing to let the truth—her truth—sink in.

That she wasn't EG Project's road manager any longer was a hard pill to swallow, but completely losing her job wasn't something she anticipated. Less than twenty-four hours ago, Amethyst Entertainment terminated her contract on the grounds of "unprofessionalism, and failing to uphold the work ethic the company wants its employees to practice."

All because someone had witnessed Yihwan kiss her in that damn stairwell, assumed it was *her* doing, and decided it was a story they needed to broadcast to the entire building.

Just her luck.

Her phone rang and she broke down upon hearing Minchan's voice singing the chorus of *Stuff of Daydreams*. It was Gabriel calling, but she ignored the phone call completely and dragged her feet on the way back to her room.

She collapsed onto her bed. It was going to be a *long* day.

Yihwan couldn't remember the last time he sat with Haera in a heavily tinted car like this one. South Korean celebrities who wanted to go on dates didn't have the freedom to step out in public without being photographed or having rumors spun about them. Hence, car dates.

They used to take two-hour rides around Seoul—sometimes chaperoned, sometimes not. Haera would bring packed meals; Yihwan would bring drinks. And they'd content themselves with watching movies or TV dramas on his iPad. Sometimes, when their crazy schedules sapped whatever was left of their energy, they'd simply fall asleep in each other's arms.

But it was awkward now, the way his body was shifted away from her, and hers from him. She was the one who had asked to see him, and he'd agreed, if only to put an end to this. Whatever this is.

When Haera spoke, Yihwan thought she sounded like she was delivering an acceptance speech, thanking him for agreeing to see her. *It's fascinating, what time apart could do to people*, he mused. Before coming here, he was convinced seeing the woman he once loved would make him feel weak in the knees, but he was wrong. He felt nothing of the sort. Not even when the smell of her perfume brought him back to the times he had his lips pressed against her skin.

"I don't know if I should thank you for throwing that bait."

"I'm not asking you to."

"Then what's this for?"

"I was sincere when I told you that I missed you, Yihwan-ah."

He believed her. He hated that he did, but it was the truth. There was no mistaking the earnestness in Haera's eyes right now. He hated that he found himself unable to look away too.

"I don't know what you want me to say, noona."

"You don't have to say anything. Just…stay with me for a little while."

⸺

"No. You *cannot* just fire someone over some bullshit reason and send her packing without even a full month's notice!"

Gabriel had stormed through the tenth floor hall, right into the interim CEO's office, demanding to have a word with the boss. He found it was only Mr. Jin who was in for work at the moment, and he naturally turned his rage toward the executive assistant. It didn't help that the EA gave him such an unsatisfying reason as to why Filipina Legaspi's contract with Amethyst was so unceremoniously terminated.

"Mr. Park, I would appreciate it if you'd mind your language."

"I'm not here to cater to *your* comfort, Mr. Jin. It's the CEO I want to see."

"Like I said," the man emphasized, clearly becoming agitated as well. "Mr. Kang is out meeting some investors. It might take a while."

He balled his hands into fists, but decided the emotional satisfaction he'd get punching Mr. Jin in the face wasn't worth losing his job for. Especially *not* when his purpose for being here was to fight for something. *Someone*. He unclenched his fists.

"I'll wait."

"Suit yourself." Mr. Jin gestured toward the waiting area. He offered Gabriel some coffee, but was quickly turned down.

As he waited, Gabriel dialed Fi's number, worried about her current emotional state. She hadn't picked up any of his calls since this morning, when he'd heard the news from Fi's sunbae.

"*I want to keep my job too*," he recalled Fi saying when she finally agreed to the reassignment. It should have been a hopeful step toward getting back on her feet, but sometimes even the universe was cruel enough to offer a place of refuge, only to lock you out of it.

He could only imagine how miserable she must feel, and he felt uneasy that all he could do was *sit and wait* until he could lobby his case to CEO Kang. He shook his head. Something about the old man didn't sit well with him when he took over as interim CEO five months into Gabriel's first year at Amethyst, and now he was beginning to see why.

He didn't have a lot of opportunities to meet the previous CEO, Kwon Jaekwan, who vacated his post temporarily to receive medical treatment overseas. But Gabriel saw enough of him, however, to know that he and CEO Kang weren't cut from the same cloth.

Kwon Jaekwan was warm and fatherly. He was someone who took time out of his schedule to meet everyone working at AmEnt every month, to speak to them not only about the business, but also about personal matters. It wasn't unheard of for CEO Kwon to send flowers to an employee who had a death in the family, or a congratulatory gift to one whose child just graduated from high school.

An anecdote Fi once told Gabriel came to mind, that of the old CEO learning how to say "Hello, how do you do?" in Filipino so he could greet Fi in her native tongue the next time they met in the halls. His laughter had been hearty when he messed up on his first attempt, she said. "It was endearing."

In stark contrast was CEO Kang's administrative style. From the first day of his tenure, Kang Hyunil, who was ten years younger than CEO Kwon, had been hell-bent on increasing AmEnt's sales. All the departments had long, rigid meetings almost every day for weeks, figuring out how to sell, sell, and sell even more. The department heads were convinced the younger leader wanted to prove something to his predecessor, but they were not entirely sold on the idea of dehumanizing the workforce to achieve it.

Still, CEO Kang managed to raise AmEnt's income by 40% in his first year. An impressive achievement, if one didn't consider the number of employees who left the company because of the organizational shift. Many believed the original principles by which AmEnt operated were obliterated by CEO Kang's administration, and they eventually moved on to working environments they felt mirrored the "old Amethyst Entertainment." Warm and nurturing, like a second home.

The EA's voice interrupted Gabriel's thoughts a while later. "Mr. Park, CEO Kang just called. He says his meeting won't end until later tonight, and he advises you to see him some other time."

Of course, Gabriel thought, he'd already expected the CEO wouldn't give him the time of day. He tried his best not to scowl at the CEO's underling, but he slammed the door as he left the room anyway. *There are other ways to resolve this issue*, he told himself.

The only thing he had to do was figure out what it was.

As an actress, Haera had learned to anticipate lines. To catch a fellow actor who's about to fumble with them. To ad-lib when necessary to save a take or make it more interesting. And like a perfectly written movie scene, Haera was anticipating something. A line or two to maybe pave the way to a happy ever after.

But "*I should go*" wasn't what she expected, so she was left fumbling for a line.

Dead air. If this were a movie, it would be the part where the soundtrack would come on, a painfully beautiful melody with words that conveyed her feelings because she was having a difficult time expressing them herself.

"Kumanhaja," Yihwan finally said. It sounded to her like a director calling "Cut!" even if she wanted the film to continue rolling. "We've hurt each other enough, noona. Let's stop now."

"Can't..." Her throat seemed to constrict as her mind gave her heart one last tug back in and up her sleeve. Breaking up with Yihwan had been a calculated choice. She could have gone on with their relationship and struggled keeping it under wraps (because God knows how the press and fans can hound you once they find out), but she followed a career path that guaranteed success instead. She had since found out it's true what they say about being lonely at the top.

"... can't we give this another try?"

"Let's not."

"Is there someone else?"

There was a pause, and Haera's heart sank to her stomach when she saw reluctance in his eyes. *So there* is *someone*, she thought. *What's she like, Yihwan-ah?*

"No, there isn't."

"Then why?"

Yihwan shook his head like he couldn't believe she was asking this question. "Do you know, noona, that I have written maybe a hundred songs about you? That I could perhaps write a hundred more?"

The words that spilled out of him brought a wave of wonderful memories—that of Yihwan's voice on the phone at two in the morning, serenading her with songs still unfinished, telling her he wrote them while thinking of her.

"I wrote songs about the way you smile, the way you walk, the way your fingers feel heavenly on my skin—all kinds of songs. All of them about you."

Her Yihwan had always been so sweet, but his words now brought a bitter taste to her mouth. Haera wanted to tell him to stop, but she figured if this was the last time she'd hear him talk about her, she'd take the bitter with the sweet.

"The world might never hear any of those songs, but I know them in my heart to be beautiful because they're yours."

"Yihwan-ah…"

"*You* are all my songs," he said, an admission that could as well have been read between the lyrics he wrote. "But you were the one who decided I should stop singing."

"I miss Fi noona," Minchan blurted out, eyes fixed on his laptop screen. In the past half hour, he'd created three different online personas and posted on EG Project fan forums that exploded with malicious content about their former road manager. He was surprised at how terribly hostile the fans were toward him when he would defend Fi's character. They even accused him of actually *being* Fi and trying desperately to clear her name.

"Me too," said Steven, who was sitting in a corner of the room, trying to polish the song Minchan wrote back in Manila.

"Do you think this will work?"

The drummer looked up from his song sheets. "Hm?"

"This YouTube thing we did." Minchan had closed the fan forum window and was now staring at their YouTube channel, at the latest video: *Song Minchan Is a Bully, Part 1*. "I mean, it's getting a lot of views, and I'm getting a lot of hate right now, but...do you think it'll work?"

"I hope it does. We have material for the next one, yeah?"

"Ne. You ready to get hurt?"

"I thought we had a disclaimer."

"I mean *emotionally.*"

When Fi woke up three hours later, more of her started to hurt. Her head, her stomach, even her neck. Feeling hungry, she shuffled toward her kitchen to find something to eat and settled for cup ramyun and a boiled egg. And as she sat in her kitchen-and-dining area, she wondered when this place began to feel so suffocating.

The studio-type apartment had been a perfect choice for her when she decided to stay in Seoul after signing with Amethyst Entertainment. It didn't have much, but it had everything she needed: a space for a nicely sized bed, a small kitchen and dining table for two, a bathroom with steady running water, and a reliable heating system for cold winter nights. Granted, it was her first time to live alone (while studying, she lived in a dorm with a female roommate from Thailand), but the place had always felt safe, comfortable.

Until that moment.

She'd probably have to move out soon, if she didn't find herself a new job in two weeks. Landlords were only as friendly as the last time you paid rent, after all. But if she did move out, she had no clue as to where she might go. Five years in Korea, and she had only lived in Seoul, and this was the cheapest, most decent place she could find.

She poured water into her ramyun cup and put it in the microwave, setting it to a minute. Her mind momentarily wandered to the moment that got her in this position in the first place. The moment she's fantasized about more than once before.

The moment Yihwan kissed her.

The band leader probably didn't know it was her first. She'd never been one to divulge information like that, after all. But what upset her more now was not that Yihwan let his emotions get the best of him, but that *it was Yihwan* who gave Fi her first kiss. And she surprised even herself—the loud *ding!* of the microwave at the right moment didn't help, either—when she realized whose lips she really wanted to kiss.

Great. Now my heart hurts too.

Text Log: Carlos Santillan & Filipina Legaspi
August 15

Carl, 4:23 pm
Ang harsh. Isn't there some kind of law about that? Or are they taking advantage because you're NOT a South Korean citizen, therefore they can dispose of you as they wish?

Fi, 4:30 pm
I'm pretty sure meron. I'm just not sure how to approach it without having to get a lawyer. I guess the best thing to do is to move on now.

Carl, 4:47 pm
Figured. Pero nakakapikon sila ha!
You've been working so hard for the past five years, Fi!
Doesn't loyalty mean anything to them?

Fi, 5:02 pm
In the grand scheme of things, money means more to them than loyalty. They've been losing a lot because of me.

Carl, 5:05 pm
Is it still because of that blind item?

Fi, 5:07 pm
You'd better believe it.

Carl, 5:15 pm
God. That's some screwed-up shit.
Anyway, Fi... if you need any help, just let me know, all right?
I have a consultation schedule in a few.

Fi, 5:19 pm
Psh. It's like you don't know me at all. I'll be fine.
Just don't tell Mom, OK?

Text Log: Gabriel Park & Jo Yihwan
August 17

Jo Yihwan, 6:30 pm
Any word from CEO Kang?

Gabriel Park, 7:15 pm
None yet, but it's just a couple of hours since
I sent the email anyway. I hope he's in
good enough shape to be able to read it, at least.

Jo Yihwan, 7:20 pm
He should be. I heard from Kijoo noona before that he's been
recuperating well. Just keeping thing quiet.

Gabriel Park, 7:24 pm
Do you mean to say there's a chance he might return?

Jo Yihwan, 7:25 pm
Don't take my word for it.

Gabriel Park, 7:30 pm
Steven and Minchan showed me an anti-bullying campaign
concept the other day. I think it's rather inspired,
said you should go for it.

Jo Ylhwan, 7:35 pm
We're working on it a bit more. I don't know if the upper
management will agree to it, but fuck that.
They aren't the only ones who can put things out there.

Gabriel Park, 7:37 pm
If you need help, I'll be on board.

Jo Ylhwan, 7:40 pm
I was waiting for you to say that.

Gabriel Park, 7:47 pm
Just let me know what you need.

Text Log: Jo Yihwan & Filipina Legaspi
August 18

Yihwan, 7:03 pm
I'm going to go ahead and assume you're mad at me
because you haven't been answering my calls since that day.
But I'm really, really sorry.

I shouldn't have done what I did, Fi. It was rude and inappropriate,
and I got you into so much trouble because of it. I am so sorry.

You're mad at me now, that's okay. I can take that. When you're
ready, I hope you'll give me a chance to see you again and tell you
all these things because this all just seems so impersonal.

I'm really sorry. Please forgive me.

Fi, 7:45 pm
I don't really know how I feel about everything, Yihwan.
To be honest, I am just so overwhelmed right now.

Apology accepted. Don't be too hard on yourself.

You have a band who relies on you,
and you need to focus so they don't stray
from what you've worked hard for.

Yihwan, 7:48 pm
How do you do that?

Fi, 7:51 pm
Do what?

Yihwan, 7:59 pm
Act like everything's fine?
Still have the mind to look out for us?

Fi, 8:13 pm
Easy. In my heart, you are family.
And you never stop looking out for family, no matter what.

TRACK FOURTEEN
ALL ON YOUR OWN

FANS TOOK TO TWITTER hours after *Song Minchan Is A Bully, Part 2* was uploaded, berating Minchan for his bratty attitude. Debates sparked on whether or not the video clips were scripted, while others either posted directly on the bassist's social media accounts or ranted among themselves in the fan forums.

Clearly, phase 1 of EG Project's plan was working, and that was a sign that they needed to continue working on a follow-through. All night, Yihwan and Steven worked together to complete the arrangement to Minchan's song—now christened *Golden*—and they were all in the studio now, recording a rough version of the song.

Are you conscious
Just how precious
You are, you are

Did they shatter you
Did they take it
Too far, too far

Like some of the band's previous rock ballads, *Golden* started slow and relaxed. Yihwan let go of his Stratocaster in favor of the keyboards, providing the gentle rhythm that opened the song. Steven worked his magic on the percussions, creating a steady pulse that crawled stealthily in the background, building up until Minchan, now on lead guitar, brought on the chorus.

When you reach the verge of breaking down
Find me
I promise to be around

Get up; I'll be with you, don't surrender to the hate
Don't let them dictate, don't let them seal your fate
You're golden (You're golden)
And it's about time you showed them

"I knew I was going to find you here."

The timbre of that voice was enough to make Fi look up from her bowl of ramyun—deer in the headlights expression, noodles hanging from her lips—and almost choke. Luckily, there was a water dispenser near the door, and Gabriel was quick to grab a tin cup, fill it with water, and hand it over to Fi.

She took the cup and drank from it slowly, watching the PR manager pull a chair from a vacant table and sit across her. From his well-pressed blue button-down to his towering height, Gabriel looked all sorts of misplaced in this rickety hole in the wall.

"How, even?"

"I thought a lot about it," Gabriel said, shrugging. "You showed me this place before, remember? When I was new at Amethyst..."

Fi was surprised he remembered, especially since they had only been here twice. The first time was when he got lost after a friendly game of street basketball and managed to wander into her neighborhood.

"Right. When you got lost around here."

"I recognized you from work, so I thought to ask for directions. But you were walking so quickly..."

"So you just followed me around like a homeless puppy."

"I had a feeling you'd take me in," he blurted out and chuckled softly. Fi's cheeks started feeling warm, and it was definitely not the ramyun. She stared into her bowl and went back to eating her meal, hoping to conceal her kilig.

Meanwhile, Gabriel scanned the restaurant with an amused smile on his face. Nothing about the place had changed, save for a few new idol posters here and there. The ahjumma running this joint seemed to be good at keeping up with current trends. The EG

Project poster on the wall near the counter was from their most recent magazine feature.

"Anyway, you weren't answering my calls. I was worried. Thought I'd give this place a shot, and here you are," he told her, putting his arms on the table and covering almost half of it. "How are you doing?"

"I'm alive."

"Filipina."

"I'll be all right. Just... maybe not today. Or tomorrow. Or the day after that."

Fi placed her wooden chopsticks down beside her bowl of ramyun and let her gaze wander around the small space she and Gabriel now shared. It wasn't a busy day; from where she was seated, she could only see one other occupied table. That left four more vacant.

She liked this place because it served cheap, tasty food, and it was conveniently near her apartment. Above all, the ahjumma running it reminded her of her mother: sweet and warm, if a bit naggy at times.

She couldn't remember if she had told Gabriel all this, but he seemed to have a good recollection of this place anyway. Perhaps it was because of the food he had, whatever that was, when they were here last.

"I feel like this is my safe place, you know? I can have meals alone and not be treated like a loser," Fi confessed with a resigned shrug. "Especially now that I feel like Cady Heron, and the entire Original fandom is my Regina George."

Gabriel propped his elbow on the table, rested his chin in his palm and just stared at her.

"I'm sorry, Regina George is—"

"I *know* who Regina George is," Gabriel cut her off, smirking. "I heard she does car commercials. *In Japan*."

She laughed. He quickly went on full defensive mode, saying it was his first girlfriend who dragged him to the movies to see *Mean Girls* when it first came out.

"That you remember lines from the movie makes me assume you didn't watch it only once."

"My cousin asked me to buy her a DVD copy for her birthday. And then she asked me to stay and watch it with her friends during her slumber party—I was really only there as a guardian."

Fi couldn't hide her amusement. "Are you always this much of a pushover?"

"Depends on how much I like the person," he replied with a smile that made Fi's heart flutter so much, she found the need to divert her attention to the side dishes in front of her. There was kimchi, odeng, and caramelized baby potatoes. Some restaurants offered six or seven banchan, but Fi could hardly demand more when she only paid for a measly bowl of ramyun.

"Fi—I want you to know that we're doing something to overrule the termination."

She looked up at him again, wide-eyed. "Oh no, you don't have to do that."

"Why not? What they did was wrong. By law, they can't just fire you like that!"

"Gabe, it's... It's just too much *work.* You have things to do, *I* have things to do—"

"Like what? You can't seriously be thinking of coming here to mope every day."

Fi shot Gabriel a look that usually shut him up, but he challenged her gaze instead, as though daring her to prove him wrong. Sighing, she picked up one of her chopsticks and started poking at the odeng, getting frustrated when she repeatedly failed to pick up a piece.

"What are you doing?"

"Heart surgery. Obviously," she snapped, flicking the chopstick up in the air like a cheap magic wand. If Gabriel had been leaning any closer, she perhaps would have poked his eye.

He didn't say anything and simply pulled his head back, eyes still trained on her.

"I now hereby declare I'm as useless as this chopstick."

A frown lined Gabriel's face as he watched her in solemn contemplation. Fi couldn't help but think he now saw crisis whenever he looked at her.

"Don't say that." He took the wooden utensil from her hand and cast an apologetic glance at it, like she'd hurt its feelings. Gabriel then used it to retrieve a piece of odeng from the side-dish plate and gloated when he succeeded. "You're just being impatient," he said, insisting the chopstick is useful for poking and picking things up. All while shoving *her* food in *his* mouth.

"Really."

"Mm-hmm," Gabriel hummed, picking up one of the baby potatoes and pretending to feed it to her, only to pull it away at the last second so he could eat it instead.

"Gabe."

"Fi..." He paused to properly chew his food. "You, of all people, are the farthest thing from being useless. There are just limitations to what you can do now because you're alone. Or you feel like you are."

He took her other chopstick. "Two together can accomplish more things. And faster," he pointed out, picking up another baby potato to really feed it to her this time. She smiled at him before taking it in her mouth.

"You know what? There was this one time Minja noona rounded everyone up at the PR Department for drinks," Gabriel narrated, moving the utensils idly in the air like some kind of university lecturer ready to point something out on the board. "I was still green then. Maybe three, four months in? And when everyone got past the tipsy point, one of the guys suggested we should play the chopstick game."

"Oh no. Not *the* chopstick game."

"Oh yes. *The* chopstick game. It was new to me, so I just went, 'What the heck,' and played along. Also I was very, very drunk and bordering on stupid," he admitted, making her laugh.

Quickly, he snatched an unused paper napkin from the dispenser and cleaned the pair of chopsticks he was holding. Five seconds later, he was holding them through three fingers—under his index, over the middle, and under the ring finger again. A squeak came out of Fi when Gabriel slammed his hand on the table, the force of his index and ring fingers crushing the chopsticks against his middle finger. He groaned and shook the pieces off his hand.

"Jesus, you didn't have to show me! I know how that game is played!"

He only laughed and eyed the bamboo container on the other table holding wrapped wooden chopsticks. Before Fi could figure out what he was thinking, Gabriel reached for the container and grabbed four pairs of chopsticks. He stuffed them between his fingers like the first time. "Do you think I can break all of this if I slam them hard enough?"

"I think you'll break your fingers."

"*Exactly.*"

Fi rolled her eyes and sighed.

Gabriel put the chopsticks back into the bamboo container and picked up the pair he broke, gazing at it sadly before locking gazes with her again.

"Do you know what I love about you, Fi? You're a force all by yourself," he told her, his earnest eyes boring into hers. Could anyone blame her if she got stuck on the word "love?"

Because she did, and there was that disconnect again between the time his lips uttered words and her ears were able to grasp them.

"... and I just don't want to see you broken. At least not on your own."

TARA FREJAS

[HEADLINE] EG Project Attracts Attention
With New Song
August 23 | Hanguk Daily

East Genesis Project released a new song today through their official YouTube channel.

Golden, penned by bassist Song Minchan, has garnered almost 300,000 views in a span of eight hours. This is the first EG Project song that the youngest member of the band has written.

The short introduction to the video post reads, "*Golden* is a song about recognizing your worth no matter what society tells you. We hope it will remind everyone that we are, all of us, precious in the eyes of the people we love and the people who love us."

Comments have been flooding the group's YouTube channel since the song was released. Fans now speculate that the song is dedicated to one of EG Project's female staff members, who has fallen prey to hostile netizens after being photographed with band leader Jo Yihwan at a hotel overseas.

Meanwhile, Amethyst Entertainment has confirmed the band's comeback with a new album in October. This will be EG Project's third Korean album since debuting in 2011.

COMMENTS

[+5,221, -3,091] The song is actually really good. I'm so proud of Minchan. He's all grown up.

[+5,002, -2,100] Daebak. They even spent time writing a song for that woman. I heard she'd been kicked out of Amethyst Entertainment already for causing so much trouble. Good riddance.

[+4,231, -1,004] I don't get why people are so mad about EG Project putting out a beautiful song with a beautiful message. These so-called fans should get a grip!

[+3,765, -908] I cried listening to the song. Brilliant job, Song Minchan!

[+3,044, -605] As expected from EG Project. This song brought me to tears. Come crawling right back, you ex-Originals!

TARA FREJAS

GOLDEN
Lyrics by Song Minchan
Music by Steven Bae, Jo Yihwan

Are you conscious
Just how precious
You are, you are

Did they shatter you
Did they take it
Too far, too far

When you reach the verge of breaking down
Find me
I promise to be around

CHORUS
Get up; I'll be with you
Don't surrender to the hate
Don't let them dictate
Don't let them seal your fate
You're golden (You're golden)
And it's about time you showed them

Are you wond'ring
Why you're nowhere else
but here, right here

Don't forget: there's
a grand design and you're
part of it, part of it

It's okay if you stumble to the ground
Find me
I will be around

Repeat Chorus

FIFTEEN

그냥 해라/JUST DO IT

CEO KANG WAS *NOT* HAPPY.

The production and release of *Golden* had been done completely behind everyone's backs. Everyone in upper management, at least. The talent heads, marketing officers, and PR managers all knew EG Project had something up their sleeves, but they'd kept mum about it until the song was unleashed onto the internet.

The band, their handlers, and the marketing and PR teams were now inside a conference room, waiting for the interim CEO to finish listening to the song on his table *and* finally breathe a word to them. As Gabriel read the room, he decided CEO Kang really didn't have anything to say. The old man merely needed to flaunt his rank, to remind everyone who was boss.

"Well…" CEO Kang sighed and put his tablet down. "It's too late to take it down, isn't it?"

"Why should we? There's nothing wrong with it." Yihwan asked back. There was no mistaking the snippiness in the band leader's tone. And before the CEO could lecture him about protocol, Yihwan continued, "It's music. It's what we *do*. We post nonsensical things in our Twitter and KakaoStory accounts every day—we didn't need to follow protocol for that, did we?"

The other people in the room nodded and whispered among themselves in agreement.

"If Minchan can post a picture of his lunch on Instagram and Steven can tell everyone on Twitter that he wants to own a dog, why can't we put something out there that actually has *meaning*? Something we actually worked hard for?"

A debate erupted between the two men, one defending the importance of a system, and the other emphasizing creative freedom. Soon, the talent heads present as well as the marketing people started to speak up. From an outsider's point of view, it would seem as if the subordinates just sparked some kind of revolution.

Gabriel had only once been in the same room with Jo Yihwan while some sort of serious discussion transpired, but now that he wasn't the one exchanging heated words with the band leader, he was impressed.

The boy had guts. He knew how to choose his words; his attack was tactful, his defense strong. Gabriel recalled asking Fi what she liked about him, and she said—after joking about how Yihwan's elbows are pretty—that there was something about his eyes, that they carried fire in them when he spoke of or did something he was passionate about.

He could see it now, the fire that enticed the moth and burned her in the end.

The discussion continued until CEO Kang conceded with a heavy sigh. "All right then. Do what you want," he said and retreated with his opinions back in his pockets. The old man awarded Gabriel an exacting look before adjourning the meeting, leaving the room shortly with his EA. Glances were exchanged across the room; it was unlike CEO Kang to just back off like that.

This might not be the end of it.

***

"It was awesome, Minchan-ah. I'm so proud of you," Fi told the EG Project magnae over the phone. On her face was a wide grin she wished he could see at the moment. "I guess that ten-song exercise really did work!"

"Among other things."

"Well, I hope it finds a spot in your next album."

"Maybe we have other plans for it," Minchan said, his tone with a tinge of mischief.

Fi was certain it wasn't Minchan's intention to make her feel cut off from everyone, but his words stung all the same. She missed planning everything with them—album concepts, costumes, what to eat after a broadcast—and it hurt to realize she was now getting information about her band *from the internet*.

Or phone calls like this.

"I miss you, noona." Minchan's voice sounded just a tad louder than a whisper now, and Fi knew he was feeling embarrassed to say it. "Justin hyung is awesome, and the rest of the staff are cool as always, but I miss you."

She managed an "Aww," and stopped there, else she let him hear her voice break.

"I'd let you pinch my cheeks whenever you want if you come back to us," Minchan added, making her laugh at his bargaining chip. Being the band magnae came with certain inconveniences, and perhaps one of the most annoying things Minchan ever had to endure was getting his cheeks pinched. It didn't help that he had rounder cheeks during their debut days.

"I stopped doing that in Japan."

"I'll let you have a go at it again. Just come back."

She wondered how much Minchan knew about the goings-on at Amethyst, or, more particularly, what had happened between Yihwan and herself that led to her termination. Yihwan wasn't the type to kiss and tell, after all. The only reason why Fi knew a lot about his relationship with Haera was because she was there to witness it.

She guessed Minchan was in the dark about a lot of things, and maybe it was better that way.

Days after *Golden* was released, the AmEnt building was abuzz with rumors of CEO Kwon soon returning to Seoul, and the energy was palpable. Old-timers were walking with an extra spring in their step, laughing more, and engaging in livelier discussions with their younger colleagues.

Meanwhile, CEO Kang sat in his car, jaw clenched while watching a live stream of an EG Project press conference on his mobile phone.

A press conference about a campaign he did not sign off on or was informed about.

A huge white banner vandalized with nasty words served as EG Project's backdrop for their press conference that afternoon. Press people and fans now shared the small space inside a rented-out café in Itaewon, all of them excited and anxious to know what the event was about. Fans cheered when the speakers began to play the band's new song, and it was utter chaos when Yihwan, Steven, and Minchan finally made their appearance. The bodyguards present as well as the event host thankfully handled the situation well, and soon, everyone was ready to listen.

Gabriel stood somewhere at the back, slightly hidden behind a few members of the press. He spied Yihwan scanning the room for a bit, stopping to nod at him. He nodded right back.

Throughout Gabriel's tenure as a PR manager, Jo Yihwan had never approached him (or anyone from the PR department) with image management concerns. The band leader had always been sure of himself and lived by his principles. In the messy world of showbusiness, he knew how to carry and express himself without causing controversy. Indeed, because Jo Yihwan fulfilled his duty as band leader so well, AmEnt never had a problem managing EG Project's image until now.

There really is a first for everything, Gabriel told himself when Yihwan approached him for a consult, and the only advice he gave the band leader was, "You carry a truth in you. Feel free to burden everyone with it."

Fi took a break from her online job hunting so she could set up her browser and live stream what Gabriel described through text as "an event at three in the afternoon." Even Yihwan told her to tune in to their YouTube channel about thirty minutes ago.

It's been a while since the band's YouTube channel had been used to stream anything. The last time was when EG Project had been sent to Japan for a year and the band decided to do an impromptu Q&A session for the Korean fans who missed them. It became an hour-long spontaneous show where Yihwan, Steven, and Minchan simply picked questions from the comments section and answered them. Some fans even posted small challenges for the group, which made the session more fun.

But this—what she was witnessing right now—was completely different from that lighthearted hour when all they did inside that hostel in Osaka was laugh over silly questions that begged to be answered.

"Please tell us about your inspiration for the song *Golden*," the host requested, and the microphone was passed on to Minchan, who sat on the far right of the table.

"Someone I hold dear to me inspired this song," the bassist began, looking to their leader, who gave him an encouraging nod. "I guess it's my way of reaching out to that person—and anyone else who's been in that situation—and saying 'Hey, you are worth more than this. And I'm here for you.'"

The host spoke again: "I've listened to the song a couple of times on the way here, and I think it's great that you guys have put out something so inspiring and empowering. And now you're starting this campaign. How did this come about?"

"The initial intention wasn't of such a grand scale, to be really honest," Steven said, taking the microphone this time. "When Minchan came up with the song, we only planned to record and release it, and... y'know, send a message to the world. But as the days passed, the reception became overwhelming. We got messages from *everywhere*, thanking us, telling us we're making a difference."

Yihwan piped in. "We realized that we were able to reach out to a *lot* more people than we'd expected, and that we could become a voice that could encourage them through their struggles."

"And a voice that could represent them too," Minchan added.

"It's basically the Golden Rule—'Do unto others as you would have them do unto you'—but with a bit of introspection," Yihwan continued, his free hand making a gesture toward his chest. "We want to encourage more people to look at themselves and appreciate how precious they are because that's really where it starts. If you plant love of self within you, eventually everything you do will be touched by that love."

"And you can never go wrong with love," said Steven.

The thought brought a smile to Fi's face. Although EG Project's music had always been heavy on messages, they usually followed a theme or story, and none of them have emphasized the importance of loving yourself yet. That phone call with Haera came to mind. *Be kinder to yourself.*

She remembered Gabriel too.

"Now let's talk about the Song Minchan videos," the host said, moving on to another topic. "Don't you think the messages you're sending your fans are a bit contradicting?"

The boys laughed, and Steven answered first. "First of all, we'd like to apologize for that. Some fans were right—it's all scripted."

The fans inside the café started whispering amongst themselves when the drummer confirmed their suspicions. Many were quick to reach for their phones and type furiously.

"It was a social experiment," Yihwan admitted, then went on to say it was Steven and Minchan's brainchild. "We wanted the fans to recognize what was wrong with the picture, and they had no qualms telling us about it. There were fans who started sending angry messages to Minchan because of his behavior toward Steven. The best part, at least for me, was when someone bravely pointed out that what Minchan was doing to Steven can't even compare to what our fans are doing to our road manager, Fi."

Collective gasps were heard from fans gathered at the cafe. Yihwan allowed the chatter go on for a good five seconds before speaking into the microphone again. "Some fans were right about that too. She was the reason for all this."

"You mean your road manager who's been on the news, for..." the host paused, as if treading this territory carefully. Yihwan nodded at him, an assurance that it was fine to be straightforward. "Sleeping with you?"

"That's correct."

Oh my god.

All of a sudden, it felt as if a bomb exploded right by Fi's ear, rendering her partly deaf as Yihwan went on to say that this campaign was conceived upon experiencing the fans' volatile hate firsthand.

The camera focused on Minchan when he spoke up. "It was too overwhelming. I think each of us, even the staff, just surrendered to the feeling of helplessness after a while. We saw how Fi noona was attacked on the Internet, and even physically! And it was really difficult to watch, especially because she's basically family."

Fi's eyes widened seeing the comments on the page come up faster. If the streaming lag was anything to go by, she'd say a lot more viewers have started tuning in.

I knew it! I knew they were doing this for that bitch!

What's so special about that road manager, anyway? Did you all date her?

I think it's really sweet what they're doing. It's one thing to realize an injustice, and another to act on it.

There is a reason why EG Project is my bias.

I don't even care if Yihwan or Steven did date that girl. The fans crossed the line, and they deserve to be punished.

I don't know how to feel about this.

The video froze, and when she refreshed it, she managed to catch the host asking Yihwan if he would like to clarify anything to the public regarding the photos that started it all.

He shook his head. "People will believe what they want to believe. If I say something now, I doubt it would be able to reverse things, so I find it useless to make clarifications about those photos.

"I do, however, feel the need to tell everyone that I deeply regret not being able to protect one of our family members. Fi had been our road manager since our debut. She was fresh out of college when she came to work for Amethyst Entertainment, away from her family and the country she grew up in.

"She's a hard worker. She woke up earlier and stayed up later than the rest of us to make sure EG Project's needs were met every single day. But always, even in the toughest and lowest of times, she managed to keep the band focused, grounded, and happy. Taking care of EG Project wasn't just a job to her. She treated us like family. The band owes her a lot, and at any given time, each of us"—Yihwan gestured to Steven and Minchan—"can sit down with you and tell you a hundred reasons why we love and appreciate her. And why we are sad that the company had decided to let her go."

Yihwan's face blurred as Fi's eyes brimmed with tears. She lifted her hands to her mouth to muffle her sobbing. Being EG Project's road manager could sometimes feel like a thankless job, but this—

"Our fans are special to us," Yihwan carried on, his eyes scanning the faces in front of him. "Without them, we wouldn't be where we are now. We owe our success to them, but we also owe the same to our staff who work tirelessly behind the scenes.

"We love you, Originals, and I apologize for letting you down this time. But even so, what some of you have said and done to Fi were completely out of line, and I personally condemn these actions. Through this campaign we've started, we sincerely hope similar cases would never have to happen again to *anyone* else."

—this was gratitude enough to make her forget all the days she'd missed meals, the nights she'd lost sleep, and the long hours in between she'd missed being home.

{ HEADLINE } EG Project Launches Anti-Bullying Campaign

August 27 | Spotlight Web Magazine

Following the surprise release of East Genesis Project's song *Golden*, the band held a press conference today to announce the launch of *Think Golden Thoughts*, an anti-bullying campaign.

During the press conference held in a small cafe in Itaewon and live streamed through EG Project's YouTube channel, the members of the band shared their thoughts about the harassment they experienced through social media during the past month. The band leader, Jo Yihwan, was in the spotlight recently for being photographed with a member of their entourage at a hotel overseas. The photos and accompanying article drove netizens and fans to think that he had engaged in sexual activity with the staff member, thus sparking a witch hunt for the woman, whom Jo identified as their road manager.

"What some of you have said and done to [our road manager] were completely out of line, and I personally condemn these actions," the band leader emphasized, adding that they started this campaign so that no other similar cases happen to anyone else.

The band is making arrangements to visit high schools and universities to bring the *Think Golden Thoughts* campaign closer to their target audience. They hope that the students will be open-minded enough to understand and imbibe the concept of "thinking more positively about themselves and others" to prevent the culture of bullying from spreading further.

COMMENTS

[+4,075, -1,281] Finally. Someone actually has the balls to tell everyone what's wrong about the society we live in. Thank you so much, EG Project. I'm your fan now.

[+3,002, -145] Just last year, three people in my high school killed themselves because they were being bullied for various reasons. I'm not an EG Project fan, but I think they're taking a step toward the right direction, and for that, I applaud them.

[+1,007, -9,091] Attention seekers. They're afraid of being thrown away by their fans, so they pull this kind of stunt. This is low even for you, Jo Yihwan.

[+1,936, -287] What I want Jo Yihwan to do is come to my school and hit all the bullies in the face with his Fender or something.

[+2,901, -889] They're doing the right thing, but how long are they going to keep this up, I wonder? Part of me wants to think they're just doing this for publicity.

Text Log: Carlos Santillan & Fi Legaspi
August 27

Carl, 6:30 pm
I hope you've seen my latest email.

Fi, 7:15 pm
I have. I'm considering it.

Carl, 7:20 pm
Seriously? That would be awesome.
Of course, there's not much money in it,
but I think you'd be able to help a lot of kids.

Fi, 7:24 pm
You say "kids" as if we're so old.
It hasn't been that long since we graduated, you know.

Carl, 7:25 pm
All these kids calling me "sir" have taken a toll on me.

Fi, 7:30 pm
Don't get carried away. SIR.

Carl, 7:35 pm
Oh, shut up. Tell me when you're coming home
so we can arrange things, okay?

Fi, 7:37 pm
See you in two days, Carl.

Text Log: Jo Yihwan & Han Haera
August 28

Han Haera, 6:30 pm
I've seen what you've been doing on the news.
I'm allowed to tell you how proud I am of you, right?

Jo Yihwan, 7:15 pm
You are.

Han Haera, 7:20 pm
Your heart has always been in the right place, anyway.
I'm glad you haven't changed all that much.
I wish you the best on that campaign.
Silently cheering for the three of you.

Jo Yihwan, 7:24 pm
Thank you, noona. I hope you're doing well shooting
your new film too. Take care of yourself.

Han Haera, 7:25 pm
That means a lot to me, Yihwan. Thank you.

Text Log: Gabriel Park & Filipina Legaspi
August 29

Gabriel Park, 2:09 pm
But I thought you were looking for a job here in Seoul.

Fi Legaspi, 2:21 pm
I've tried. It didn't work out as well as I'd hoped.
Can't afford to live in my apartment any longer either,
so I'm going back home for a while.

Gabriel Park, 2:26 pm
When are you leaving?

Fi Legaspi, 2:27 pm
Tomorrow.

Gabriel Park, 2:32 pm
Already?

Fi Legaspi, 2:35 pm
All my bags are packed, I'm ready to go.

Gabriel Park, 2:39 pm
Oh no, you're not luring me into singing that.

Fi Legaspi, 2:41 pm
I'm standing here outside your door.

Gabriel Park, 2:44 pm
You'd better not be. I'm not home. And that's creepy.

Fi Legaspi, 2:45 pm
I hate to wake you up to say goodbye.

Gabriel Park, 2:47 pm
Already awake.

Fi Legaspi, 2:49 pm
But the dawn is breaking, it's early morn.

Gabriel Park, 2:50 pm
Can we have a decent conversation here?

Fi Legaspi, 2:53 pm
The taxi's waiting, he's blowing his horn.

Gabriel Park, 2:54 pm
Already I'm so lonesome, I could die.
Damn it.

Fi Legaspi, 3:02 pm
Thanks for everything.
Look after the kids when I'm gone.

Gabriel Park, 3:05 pm
Not funny.

Fi Legaspi, 3:15 pm
You know what?

Gabriel Park, 3:17 pm
What?

Fi Legaspi, 3:23 pm
It feels good not to be a lonely chopstick.
Thank you for always being there for me. <3

TRACK SIXTEEN

CHIN UP

*T*HREE WEEKS LATER.

"I had to be practical. Of course I'm still sad that I lost my job, but everything was so sudden that I really wasn't able to prepare myself. Financially, most of all."

"Don't you have money saved up?"

"I do, but it can only go so far. Living in Seoul isn't exactly cheap... and you know I send Mom half my salary every time."

Carlos sighed and handed Fi her cup of coffee, saying nothing else. They'd stopped by a nearby cafe on the way to their high school alma mater, where Fi was invited to speak about bullying to a room full of freshmen. At first, she wasn't convinced she'd make an effective resource person, but Carlos said she only needed to be sincere, to speak from the heart.

An hour later, she opened her speech *Mean Girls* style:

"Everyone close your eyes. Raise your hand if you've ever been bullied, whether physically or verbally, by anyone in this room." She waited around ten seconds and said, "Open your eyes."

There was a buzz inside the auditorium; a good majority of the attendees realized they've all fallen victim to bullying. Fi commanded their attention again, asking them to close their eyes once more and, "Raise your hands if you have ever said or done anything unpleasant about your friend, whether they were aware of it or not."

There was a reluctant show of hands. Fi waited a little longer this time until she felt she was looking at the same number as the first time.

"Open your eyes."

The whispering grew louder, and Fi allowed the students a few seconds to let things sink in.

"I like that a lot of you were honest and brave enough to raise your hands for the second question. I didn't think there'd be that many, but for that, I applaud you." She clapped her hands and encouraged everyone to do the same until the walls of the auditorium echoed their applause.

"You might be wondering why there should be some kind of talk about bullying when we already know that it's bad. But *only* knowing it is precisely why we need this kind of talk. There's a difference between only knowing what is bad and *doing* something about it."

As she continued with her speech, Fi spotted Carlos—fist raised, and with a proud smile across his face—watching her from the far end of the room. She smiled at him in return, thankful for a friend who always had her back, thousands of miles away or otherwise.

Back in Seoul, EG Project's advocacy work continued right on the heels of completing their Asian tour. Coordinating closely with educators, they visited schools and talked to students about the *Think Golden Thoughts* campaign, offering a mini concert at each stop. Their song *Golden* also became a massive hit, hitting a hundred thousand downloads on the first day of digital release alone.

"On top of that, netizen backlash seems to have begun fading into oblivion," Gabriel happily reported during a regular alignment meeting with the band and their staff. "The public's opinion about EG Project have been mostly positive so far, and we're glad to say that Originals from all over the world have been contacting us about activities they have been organizing to show support for *Think Golden Thoughts*. We're collecting all of the information right now and handing it over to you boys once we're done."

"Good job, guys," Justin said, clapping the shoulder of the band member closest to him, Yihwan.

"Couldn't have done it without you," Yihwan replied. Steven and Minchan nod in agreement.

"You think CEO Kang will finally be happy with the way things are turning out?" Minchan asked. It was a hypothetical question that made everyone present laugh, albeit softly.

The truth was that the interim CEO was already feeling the rug getting pulled out from underneath his feet ever since the rumors about CEO Kwon returning became fact. The older man was set to arrive in Seoul in a couple of weeks, and CEO Kang is, in a manner of speaking, threatened.

"Who cares about CEO Kang?" Steven scoffed. "Has anyone spoken to Fi lately?"

A brief silence spread across the room. Gabriel saw Yihwan throw a glance at him, but neither of them spoke up.

"I have!" Minchan excitedly replied. "She said she doesn't have a permanent job yet, but it's amazing that she gets to do these anti-bullying talks at her old school."

Gabriel smiled, recalling how, during their last phone call, Fi had sounded so worried about standing in front of a crowd and talking to them about something so personal and so recent.

"So she's basically doing what *we're* doing?" Steven asked.

Minchan nodded. "Yup! Isn't it great?"

"Gosh, I miss her a lot," the drummer mused. His gaze fell on Justin, and he quickly said, "No offense, Justin. It's just... Let's be real. We're all guys here and we're kind of sick of each other's faces."

Justin laughed and waved his hand dismissively. "None taken. I get it."

"So, are we done here?" Yihwan finally asked, checking his watch.

"Yes, we are," Gabriel replied and started clearing the space in front of him while everyone else left their seats. As he shut down his laptop, he looked up to realize Yihwan had been standing there, angling for a handshake. He obliged. "Got somewhere you have to be?"

"Anniyo. Song number 10 is just calling to me. I have to get to it before I forget."

"Oh. For the new album, right?"

"Yeah. Schedule's tight, but I think we're good."

Both Gabriel and Yihwan left the room after everyone else, chatting on their way to the elevators. "What about that special concert you're planning?" Gabriel asked. "Don't think we've been updated about it."

"Oh that's definitely happening. We'll let you know once we've finished planning it. You should come get some drinks with us sometime. That's when all the magic happens."

Gabriel laughed as the elevator doors opened. Both men stepped inside and pressed the buttons to their respective floors; Yihwan to the seventh, Gabriel to the fifth. "I'm just going to take your word for it. I'm leaving the country for a couple of days."

"Oh." Yihwan stepped out when the doors opened on the seventh floor. "Where are you going?"

Gabriel only responded to him with a smile.

"Anak..."

Fi looked up from her job listings to see her mom peek through her bedroom door. "You have a package delivery downstairs."

Her brows creased in confusion. She wasn't expecting any package. "But I didn't order anything..."

Her mother only shrugged and walked away.

Scratching her head, Fi left her desk and made her way to the door, tying her unruly morning hair up in a bun. But when she opened the door to receive the supposed package, she saw Gabriel standing there, smile shining like the sun, and panicked.

She slammed the door in his face.

A knock. "...Fi?"

Jesus. God. I haven't even washed my face yet, ugh! I swear to God, Gabriel Park. "What are you even doing here?" she asked, back pressed flat against the door as if she was trying to keep the big bad wolf from coming in.

"Delivering a package."

"Last time I checked, you were a PR manager, not a messenger."

"Are you mad at me or something? Why are we talking like this?"

"Because it's the morning and I'm a mess?"

"I'd prefer the mess over a door."

It was quiet for about a minute, and Fi pressed her ear against the door for a second before pulling the door open. Her eyes widened when Gabriel, who apparently was leaning against the door, tipped over and fell on the floor.

She laughed.

"Thanks so much for giving me a hand," Gabriel muttered as he got up, making her laugh a little more. The awkwardness returned, however, when she realized they were standing in a small space between the door and the living room. Without wasting any more time, Gabriel simply pulled a package wrapped in brown paper out of his bag and handed it to her.

"As I was saying…"

"What is this?"

"Just open it."

A shake of the head and a click of the tongue later, Fi had unwrapped the package and found herself staring at a g.o.d. Chapter 4 album, signed in silver ink by all five members. Her breath caught in her throat as she examined each signature—running her fingers over each name: Joon, Kyesang, Hoyoung, Danny, and Taewoo—in awe.

"How did you get this?"

"What do you mean? The album's not out of circulation."

"I meant *the autographs*."

"I… made a few calls," he said casually.

"The truth, Gabe."

"What—it's the truth! I made a few calls to JYP, asked if I could have an album signed by all five members, and…well, it took some time before I got each signature, so."

"You actually *met* them?"

"Yes. I have photos in case you say 'pics or it didn't happen.'"

She clutched the album to her chest and looked up at him in tears. Apart from the movement EG Project began in Seoul, this was the first time in a long while someone went out of their way to do something nice for her. Her heart swelled with happiness. "Thank you so much, Gabe. This is amazing."

The corners of Gabriel's lips curled upward as he lifted one hand to the back of his head. It was as if he was embarrassed of what he was going to say next. "I listened to the song you told me about."

"Did you like it?"

"Maybe."

"There's no *maybe*. You either like it or you don't."

"Well, the song talked about roads..."

"And?"

"I'd like it if you'd tell me you're coming to take the same road with me."

He produced a brown envelope from his bag and handed it to her. Fi didn't have to ask. The AmEnt logo on the envelope gave it away.

She clutched the envelope to her chest. While thankful that the company's doors were still open for her, she wasn't sure she was ready to return to *that world* just yet. "I think... I'll stay here for the meantime."

"This is the road you want to take?"

"For now."

Gabriel nodded, but continued to lobby his case, albeit weakly. "Things are changing back there, you know. I think this entire mess became an eye opener to everyone at AmEnt, and, well...I think it's safe to say things are getting better."

"That's good to know," Fi said, a bright smile appearing on her face. Returning to Amethyst Entertainment was an opportunity she knew she shouldn't pass up, but she felt as though she needed to work on herself more now. To pay attention to herself a little more before exhausting her efforts toward another person or group of people once again. She loved her job—no doubt about it—but she made the mistake of allowing it to drown out all the self-respect she had. "But I'll pass."

"Okay, then..." Gabriel cleared his throat. "I guess I should go catch the next flight back now."

"What? Did you fly here just to tell me this?"

"Yeah. And, well. There's *that.*"

The timid way Gabriel pointed to the CD Fi now held made it difficult for her to keep her smile modest. "You really *are* this much of a pushover!"

"I told you. It depends on how much I like a person."

"But you could've texted me. You could've sent this CD through a courier!"

"I needed to see you."

Something in her head broke down when she heard him utter those words, and the smile on her face faded until she managed to blurt out: "Skype!"

Gabriel took a step forward. She took in a breath.

"That's true." His quiet, tender voice reminded her of that afternoon they spent watching the sunset at the bay. And his eyes—*oh god, those eyes!* Why did they look at her like he saw no one else but her? "But I can't do this over Skype," he whispered, bringing a hand to her face.

"Y-yeah. You c—" He leaned in slowly—*very* slowly, like he was giving her a chance to step back, push him away, kick his balls, whatever—but she remained still until he placed a kiss on her forehead. "—can't do that. On Skype," she stammered, certain her cheeks were now a bright shade of red.

"This too," he said and slowly lifted her chin up. He must have seen the crimson on her cheeks, because he grinned like he was pleased with himself before kissing the tip of her nose.

"Gabe..." His name left her lips, soft and silent, like a reluctant prayer still needing to be heard. And maybe it was a prayer. For his gaze—*this gaze*, the one she had only ever encountered from an unwilling spectator's point-of-view—to linger on her just a few seconds longer.

"Filipina."

Everything about Gabriel started to overwhelm her when he called her name, every syllable uttered with affection. And then, there was the feel of his warm hand brushing across her cheek, fingers grazing her ear until his palm meets the nape of her neck. There was the sight of his Adam's apple quivering as he spoke, and the familiar scent of him she wouldn't soon forget: wood musk with a faint hint of citrus, his cologne.

"You're my *What If*," he continued. "And I don't want that question hanging over my head any longer."

Closing the gap between them, his lips sought an answer in the form of a kiss. Tentative yet tender, and given twice. Without hesitation, she kissed him back.

It was the response he wanted, if the smile that appeared on his lips was anything to go by.

Fi smiled too. She was glad it was Gabriel this time around.

NEWS REPORT
Channel 8
October 24 | Manila, Philippines

[Establishing shot of a university's campus grounds where huge banners with the words *Free Fall Festival* are installed everywhere. Quick situationers of people setting up the stage, entering the venue, and watching the show appear on screen during the introductory voice-over.]

ELISE BONIFACIO: College students and music fans alike trooped to the annual Free Fall Festival last night to celebrate the music and creativity of our young Filipino artists. This year, festival attendees who are avid KPop fans got a surprise treat when South Korean pop-rock band East Genesis Project took the stage for a short set.

[Video clip of EG Project performing *Golden* on stage.]

CAPTION: South Korean band EG Project performs at the annual Free Fall Festival

[Video clip of Jo Yihwan]

CAPTION: Jo Yihwan, East Genesis Project guitarist and band leader

ELISE BONIFACIO: How did you end up being part of the Free Fall Festival lineup?

JO YIHWAN: (English subs on screen) We were doing some meet-and-greet events and showcases across Southeast Asia in connection with the anti-bullying campaign we started several weeks ago. Somewhere along the way, we got contacted by the organizers of the Free Fall Festival... and we're just happy to be back in Manila to

139

finally perform in front of the Filipino
audience!

ELISE BONIFACIO: Speaking of your anti-bullying
advocacy, how's that coming along?

JO YIHWAN: (English subs on screen) The
experience has been great! Back in Korea, we've
been visiting schools like this one to spread
the word about it. We perform some songs, we
bring resource people to talk about the bullying
culture and to really just encourage the younger
generation to speak out against it and help stop
it. In terms of substantial changes, I think we
still have a long journey ahead of us, but we're
just taking it one step at a time and hoping we
make a difference.

ELISE BONIFACIO: When are you returning for a
full EG Project concert?

JO YIHWAN: (English subs on screen)
Unfortunately, the Leap of Faith tour has
already ended and we don't know yet when a next
tour will happen, but Manila is definitely going
to be in the itinerary! We'll see you soon,
FilOriginals! Mahal namin kayo!

[Video footage of EG Project performing *Stuff
of Daydreams* on stage as people sing along.]

ELISE BONIFACIO: Two months ago, EG Project came
to the country for the Manila leg of their Leap
of Faith concert tour, but Typhoon Choleng
prevented the event from pushing through. Thanks
to the Free Fall Festival, fans of the band were
able to catch a quick set before the official
festival performers—Blue Popcorn, Tagay Tayo,
Staccato Flavor, and Trainman—lit the stage up
with their performances. EG Project promises to
treat their fans to a new album very soon.

Elise Bonifacio, Channel 8 News.

Amethyst Entertainment's CEO
Kwon Jaekwan Back on Board
November 20 | Korea Business Daily

Amethyst Entertainment recently announced the return of founder and CEO Kwon Jaekwan after an almost two-year hiatus.

Shortly after being diagnosed with stage 1 lung cancer, Kwon flew to the United States for treatment, leaving the agency under the care of good friend and colleague, Kang Hyunil. Kang was then AmEnt's assistant COO at the time.

Shin Minja, chief of AmEnt's PR Department, stated, "News of CEO Kwon's return could not have come at a better time. It's not a secret to the public how Amethyst Entertainment suffered several setbacks this year, and we hope that we'll be able to pick up the pieces again under his guidance."

From CEO Kwon's departure two years ago, Amethyst Entertainment suffered up to 1.5B won in losses. It was only last year that the agency began raking in decent income, with their biggest artist, EG Project, acclimating to the Japanese music industry and putting out huge-selling singles one after the other. This was followed by the smashing success of the band's six-city tour, which ran from April to May of this year. Two other artists—five-member girl group Silverazzi and rap duo Teq&Tea—also debuted during Kang's tenure.

In June, however, EG Project's leader Jo Yihwan was involved in a string of controversies, resulting in a stock drop for Amethyst Entertainment. The band is only now regaining the trust of their fanbase with the launch of *Think Golden Thoughts*, an anti-bullying campaign.

CEO Kwon is expected to officially return to his post later this week.

COMMENTS

[+5,301, -1,781] I don't know what this means for EG Project, but I'm pretty sure a lot of Originals are still mad at the other CEO for sending the band to Japan at the height of their popularity in Korea.

[+4,120, -904] Welcome back, CEO Kwon! The Originals have missed you!

[+3,907, -463] Without CEO Kwon, there'd be no EG Project. We're so happy to know that he's well enough to return where he really belongs. It did seem that CEO Kang was just all about money.

[+2,038, -942] I heard from the grapevine that CEO Kwon returned because CEO Kang's administrative decisions suck. Like Amethyst actually lost good employees because they couldn't stand CEO Kang calling the shots.

[+951 , -105] I hope this bodes well for Amethyst in general. I really like Silverazzi's style, but the songs they've put out so far are so mediocre apart from their first single. It's disappointing to see such talent go to waste.

NAVER SEARCH | EG Project

POPULAR SEARCH RESULTS

Think Golden Thoughts Goes to Schools | 3 months ago

Of Music and Soothing the Savage Beast | 3 months ago

EG Project to Receive Special Citation for *Think Golden Thoughts* |
2 months ago

EG Project Unveils New Album, Scandalized | 1 month ago

EG Project's Scandalized Achieves All-Kill | 1 month ago

Think Golden Thoughts Spreads across Asia | 1 month ago

Diamond Disk Awards Announces Nominees | 1 month ago

Song Minchan on success of *Golden*: "It still feels like a dream" | 1
month ago

EG Project Holds Showcase for Scandalized Promotions | 3 weeks
ago

Scandalized Showcase Attracts Fans from All Over the World | 3
weeks ago

The *Think Golden Thoughts* Effect: Less Hurt, More Kindness | 2
weeks ago

Think Golden Thoughts: The Little Anti-Bullying Campaign That
Could | 2 weeks ago

TARA FREJAS

This Is What a Comeback Looks Like:
EG Project Wins Major Award at the DDAs
December 31 | Naver Music

Three-member rock band East Genesis Project won
Artist of the Year and Album of the Year at the
recently concluded Diamond Disk Awards. This is
the second time the band has received both
awards, the first time being three years ago,
after the smashing success of their second
album, *Sophomore Year*.

The band, composed of Jo Yihwan (lead
guitar/piano, backup vocals), Steven Bae
(percussions), and Song Minchan (lead vocals,
bass) proudly accepted the awards tonight,
tearfully thanking the fans for their continuous
and unwavering support. In his speech, Jo Yihwan
said, "It will always be a pleasure writing
music for the fans who believe in us through
still and rough waters. Thank you for trusting
us this much, thank you for staying."

It's not a secret to the entertainment
industry how rough this year had been for the
band, their fifteen-month absence from Korean
soil making critics doubt their ability to sell
as well as they did during their first two
years. And while the initial ticket sales for
their Asian tour boded well, that phase was
riddled with scandals involving band leader Jo
Yihwan.

"A lot of people around us were doubtful we'd
win anything tonight, and that was fine. It's
been a rough year," Steven Bae disclosed at a
backstage interview. "But I guess that's what
makes this victory so much sweeter."

EG Project's newest album *Scandalized* still
remains at the top five of the local charts

144

almost three months after its release. According to Amethyst Entertainment, talks about another concert tour are underway and may perhaps push through this coming spring.

COMMENTS

[+9,251, -5,103] I never doubted EG Project for one second. These boys are everything. Congratulations, and may the new year be kinder!

[+7,045, -2,002] What a turnaround. Three months ago, my friends and I were predicting EG Project will just disappear into oblivion after that sex scandal. Mad props for coming back strong.

[+5,878, -3,345] Off-topic, but is it weird that I'm kind of shipping Yihwan with that road manager girl they photographed him with?

[+4,750, -123] If *Scandalized* didn't win Album of the Year, it would have been a travesty. It was SO good, better than their first two albums, which I loved too.

[+310, -2,890] Let's be real. They only got Artist of the Year because of that shit advocacy thing they started.

TRACK SEVENTEEN

SEASON OF CHANGE

THEY SCHEDULED A VIDEO CALL at three in the morning, New Year's day. The boys, still wearing stage makeup, were loud and rowdy, just as Fi expected them to be. She live streamed the award show, she said, and they were ecstatic to hear it. They also had loads of fun teasing Steven, who cried buckets during the acceptance speech.

"Hey, those were manly tears!" he protested, swiping a slice of pizza from Minchan and consequently starting a wrestling match behind Yihwan.

"Aren't you going to play referee?" Fi asked, concerned. Minchan seemed to have arm-barred Steven, but her vantage point couldn't help confirm it.

"Nah. We both know who's going to win anyway."

She laughed. "Are you the only ones celebrating over there?"

"Yeah. It's the New Year—everyone else is home with their families."

"Everyone except the three of you."

Yihwan shrugged and drank something from a mug. Something she supposed wasn't coffee or tea, considering the occasion. "You were here last year too."

"Yeah. I kind of miss it."

Something suddenly crashed in the background. It looked as if Steven and Minchan wandered off to the kitchen and continued their physical squabbling there.

"Scratch that," she said as an afterthought. Yihwan craned his neck and yelled for his two members to "stop that or bring it outside."

The band leader excused himself, and Fi simply gestured for him to get it over and done with. With Yihwan out of the way, she could see as much of the band's living space as the camera allowed. Seeing the EG Project dorm like this gave her a strange feeling of nostalgia, like she hadn't been there in years.

The laptop, she assumed, was sitting on the edge of the glass table because she had a clear view of the music space. She frowned at the sight of misplaced musical instruments, tangled cables, and sheets of paper on the floor. *You're not their manager anymore, Fi. Stop it*, she reminded herself.

Instead, she chose to recall the many long nights they spent in that very space, working on songs, arguing about musical arrangement, stuffing their face with food, catching Zs. She smiled, remembering Steven dozing off on his "throne," falling backward and hitting the cymbal stands. Minchan obsessively tuning his and Yihwan's guitars while a chicken wing dangled between his lips. And Yihwan randomly stopping rehearsal to pick up a pen and paper because a new song came to him and he "didn't want to lose it."

"Sorry for taking so long," Yihwan said when he returned and sat in front of the camera.

"Did you have to mop up blood?"

"Almost." He chuckled as Steven and Minchan appeared behind him, both holding a box of pizza. Apparently, the way to get the kids to stop quarrelling was to feed them. "So how have you been doing?"

"I'm all right. You know what, my alma mater had signed up to be one of the schools participating in the *Think Golden Thoughts* campaign, and I'm one of their resource speakers," Fi enthusiastically shared. "We've gotten several more resource speakers, and we're moving on to cover more schools in the area. It's been great."

"I'm sure it is," Yihwan said. "I'm really proud of you, Fi."

"Just taking a page from your book, you know. And I feel much prouder of the three of you. I wish I could've been there too."

"Well..." Yihwan threw a glance at Minchan, who was chewing on his pizza. "You are the heart and soul of *Golden*, so I guess it's safe to say you've always been with us."

The magnae lifted a thumb up in agreement, while Steven shoved Yihwan's face a bit to the side so he can hog the camera a bit. "Being with us in spirit kind of sucks though," the drummer complained. "When are you coming back?"

"I'm still thinking about it."

"You didn't already get a job there, did you?" Steven asked, sounding like a jealous boyfriend.

Fi chuckled and shook her head. "I have these talks, and that's it. You can hardly call it a job." She did get a little compensation for being a resource speaker, but it was incomparable to her AmEnt paycheck. Still, it was enough to get by on for the meantime. It wasn't like she was rushing to get a new job at the moment, either, especially after her mother encouraged her to get some rest. She had been working for five years straight, after all.

"What do we need to do to get you back on board? Go on, humor me." It was still Steven, talking like he owned Amethyst Entertainment and could afford to give Fi whatever she asked for.

"Double my last paycheck!" she joked.

"Done! I'm sure we can lobby that with CEO Kwon, right?" Steven clapped and looked to his band leader, who, in turn, shoved him away and said, "*You* lobby that yourself."

"Did you hear that, Fi? That was the sound of Yihwan's utter lack of effort."

Yihwan grabbed the throw pillow he had been sitting on and quickly whacked Steven with it, sending the drummer running away again. Fi managed to catch Steven yell "And you call yourself a band leader!" before Yihwan excused himself to chase after him.

Minchan rolled his eyes. "Kids."

Oh, you boys. Never change.

February meant school would be out for the summer soon, which also meant busy days for everyone working in the academe. Carlos was constantly stuck at his desk these days, processing a zillion student documents. On one such afternoon, Fi arrived at his office, bringing along a bunch of snacks. Carlos let out a happy sigh when he saw his friend walk in. "I'd been wondering why my Fi senses were tingling..."

"*Pft.* Fi senses—what, even?" Her eyes fell on the pile of folders on his cluttered desk. "I seem to remember this same pile from last week."

Carlos threw her an exasperated look. "Believe me, this is a completely different pile."

"Well, I'm glad I brought something for you to eat. You look like you need a lot of sustenance." She threw the bag at him, and his varsity player reflexes resurfaced when he caught it effortlessly.

He held the bag against his chest and wore a touched expression. "Aww, mahal mo talaga ako."

"May bayad yan."

A laugh. "Ginagantihan mo ako, ah."

"I think I'm ready to go back to Seoul," she declared as she sat on one of the chairs in front of her friend's desk. The sight of his name plate—*Carlos Santillan Jr., Guidance Counselor*—peeking out from underneath the mess made her heart smile with pride.

Time seems enchanted between people who have been friends for a long time; no one really grows older than when you'd last seen them, and you're always under the impression they're the same person you've known five, ten, even fifteen years ago. That was how Fi felt with Carlos. After being away from home a long while, seeing him again, working with him, and walking the same old corridors with him brought back so many warm, wonderful memories. He was the same old friend who had chosen to carve a path for himself, and from the few months she had seen him do his job, she'd say he was doing a pretty good job.

Fi had decided on her own path years ago, and even when she struggled to stay on it, she knew it was one she would never give up on. The monkey wrench life threw into her plans could have derailed her for a while, but she didn't want it to keep her off the track anymore.

Yes, there was fulfillment in representing an advocacy she believed in. For every student, teacher, and parent who approached her with their stories dealing with bullying and how it had affected their lives, Fi felt a sense of belonging. She was happy to have been able to tell her story. To inspire them, to encourage them to be stronger and braver in the face of people and circumstances that oppressed them.

Her side trip had been amazing, but it was time to get back on track.

"I know I'm going to sound impossible, but my heart still longs for that seemingly thankless job back there," she mumbled as her friend looked on. "When we were doing the talks, I asked the students once what they thought road managers did. Do you know what they said?"

"That you carry artists' things, drive them to places, and bring them coffee."

Fi nodded, grinning. "It's actually pretty accurate, if you think about it...but my job requires way more than that. I don't know if my boys were just too generous that they've let me become a part of every endeavor they made, but I *was* part of it, one way or another. It's why, when I hear their fans say EG Project's music inspired them to write, to play music, to be a better person...I feel like I've done my job well."

"You have. It's just that unfortunate things happened..."

She shrugged. "What doesn't kill you makes you stronger. And braver. And smarter."

Carlos leaned forward a bit, and like this, they looked like student and counselor now. Amusing, since he had usually been the one to ask Fi for advice when they were teens. "Well...are you stronger, braver, and smarter now?"

"I guess I am. I mean, why else would I decide to go back there?"

"I don't know—there could be a boy."

"Carlos!" Fi picked up an eraser on the table and chucked it at her friend. "Of all the things..."

The guidance counselor dodged the object and shrugged. "Aba, malay ko! Gabriel definitely made a strong case for himself, coming here to spend Christmas with you."

Fi scowled at him, although certain her friend would have already caught the red on her cheeks. "Pwede ba, I'm being serious here."

"All right, fine." Carlos pursed his lips so he could keep himself from laughing. "And you're telling me all this because... ?"

"Because I won't be able to do these talks for you anymore."

"Fi, I only asked for a favor. And, as always, you went above and beyond the call of duty. I couldn't be more thankful."

"I've learned a lot. I'm thankful for that too."

He narrowed his eyes at her. "Wait. Is Tita Diana still clueless about everything that's happened?"

"Nah, she knows. I told her over the holidays—figured it was a good enough time to tell her."

"And what did she say?"

"Oh, let's just say I'm so glad that one, most of the mean things said about me were in Korean, and two, Gabriel was around to distract her with his face...or I might have had a harder time pacifying her."

As March rolled in, so did news about Gabriel's promotion to deputy chief of the PR department. But while the majority of his team congratulated him on his new assignment, there were employees who sourgraped about it, spreading rumors about him sucking up to the recently reinstated CEO Kwon for the post.

It wasn't a completely unfounded rumor.

After Fi's dismissal from Amethyst Entertainment, one of the things Gabriel did was to consult Minja about it, and they had decided it was best to try getting in touch with CEO Kwon. He knew he probably sounded like a kid whining to a parent, but someone had to call the old man's attention to what was going on. Especially after he had discovered Fi wasn't the first to experience such undeserved treatment during CEO Kang's tenure.

Sending CEO Kwon that e-mail was a shot to the moon. Given how private the old CEO was, no one at AmEnt could tell Gabriel exactly how the old man was doing or where he was staying, only that his old office e-mail was still active.

One reply merited another, and another, and another. Soon, Kwon Jaekwan was making calls to Seoul, asking people what the hell was going on in his company. It had become apparent that whatever news CEO Kwon had been getting about AmEnt had not included issues in the workforce. It was very typical of CEO Kang to be all about results and nothing else; it just didn't occur to Gabriel how it was hurting Amethyst as a whole.

Eventually, he had been the one to unveil the ugly truth.

"So, are you ready to see your new cell?" Minja asked him with a playful chuckle the day Gabriel was scheduled to transfer to a shiny new office just several strides away from his old desk.

"Ha. Ha."

"You don't seem too happy."

"Just a little nervous. I feel like everyone's eyes are on me."

"All the women on this floor have had their eyes on you since you came here four years ago. You're still not used to it?"

"Sunbae, you know that's not what I meant."

Minja sighed and leaned against his desk the way she normally did when she was about to lecture him on something. "Gabriel, do you have any idea how big of a shift you created in just a few months? The reason why people are and will be watching your every move from now on is because they're thankful. And expecting greater things from you. I mean, you pretty much started a movement to overthrow the previous regime."

"You make it sound like CEO Kang was some kind of evil overlord or something."

"He wasn't. That doesn't mean he didn't do some questionable things that drove some of our best employees away," Minja pointed out. "Clearly, a lot of people were too scared to say anything. But you weren't."

"Not to *overthrow* him or anything like that. I only wanted to set things straight about Fi."

The tinge of mischief Minja's smile was unmistakable as she nodded at him sagely. "I guess it's true what they say about love— oh, what was it? About moving mountains?"

Gabriel scratches his eyebrow. "I think you're talking about faith, sunbae."

"Whatever. Love moves mountains, end of discussion," Minja insisted, waving her hand dismissively. "Now move your ass to your new office so we can start ironing out Q2 and Q3 plans. Chop chop!"

Minja casually walked away and approached another hoobae's table. Gabriel took his box and left his desk in favor of his new office, and on the way there, he was greeted with smiles, thumbs-ups, and other congratulatory gestures.

And yet, all he could think of was how Fi would have greeted him if she had known. Oh, how he wished she were here.

TARA FREJAS

Untitled Video
Concert AVP #4: Intro to *Golden*
TRT: 1min 30secs

0:10   [Headshot of a female high school student in uniform against a black background. CAPTION: Kim Jimin, 17. Bullied for being "a nerd."]
"Every day at school is always a struggle. Sometimes I want to skip class because the other kids bully me into doing their assignments for them. Either that or they make fun of the books I'd read."

0:22   [Headshot of a male college student against a black background. CAPTION: Yoon Raewon, 21. High school bully.]
"It's the laughter that did it for me. I made fun of someone and a lot of people laughed. It got kind of addicting—I didn't know how much hurt I'd caused other people until one of them tried to kill herself on campus. I called her Piggy."

0:35   [Headshot of a middle-aged woman against a black background. CAPTION: Margaret Lee, 46. Educator.]
"Never in my life did I think I'd cry over students making fun of the way I dress. It got worse day after day, until I felt like my students weren't interested in learning anything from me anymore, just because they were so fixated on my fashion choices. In the middle of class, I just stepped out and didn't return. I hid away in the ladies' room, crying my heart out."

0:51   [Headshot of an old man against a black background. CAPTION: Hong Jungmin, 59. Banker, father of three.]
"I think that it's okay for your children to be scared of you, but for them to not feel safe around you because you choose to ridicule them for the mistakes they make, that's not okay. I did that to my own children, and even though they've told me they've forgiven me for it, I regret it to this day."

1:12   [Interspersing words, white over black.

Bullies have many faces
but no one deserves to see them.

Your neighbor, classmate, friend,
that stranger down the street...
they are precious to other people too,
just as you are to the people who love you.]

BONUS TRACK

HOMECOMING

"**H**EY EVERYONE, I have an announcement to make..."

Three heads bent over an iPad simultaneously looked up. In the middle was Yihwan, now with unkempt auburn hair he had yet to get used to. He was holding the gadget in his hands while red-haired Steven had his chin perched on the band leader's right shoulder. Minchan sat on Yihwan's left, munching on some chips while watching the newly edited batch of AVPs they were planning to show during their upcoming concert showcase. They all looked at Justin with varying levels of curiosity, but only Steven spoke up.

"Are you dating that girl from Marketing? The one with the blonde hair and pretty eyelashes?"

Justin's jaw hung for a quick second before he cleared his throat. "As of today, I have been permanently assigned to Silverazzi and will be taking on the task of being their senior manager."

"Wait, don't you think this is a bad time to transition?" Yihwan said, apprehensive. "We're having a concert showcase in a few weeks, hyung!"

"I know. I *know.* You don't have to worry. My replacement is very efficient. Quick thinker. Very hardworking."

The boys groaned, and Justin laughed at the collective sound of frustration. He went to open the door and poked his head out, nodding to someone in the hall. "They're ready for you, I guess."

With a resigned sigh, Yihwan put the gadget away and got up from his seat as the door opened wider. Steven and Minchan did the same, but only halfheartedly.

But all that changed when Fi walked into the room, wearing a wide smile. "You sounded disappointed from behind the door."

All three yelled like South Korea had just won the FIFA World Cup Series, and Justin took this opportunity to slip out of the room unnoticed. Steven almost tripped over his own feet trying to get to Fi, while Minchan made a dash toward her for a hug. Yihwan couldn't believe his eyes. He was the last one to approach her, taking in the sight of her like he couldn't get enough of it.

"Nice hair," was the first thing she said to him.

"I hate it."

"It suits you."

"Stop flirting with Yihwan while I'm hugging you!" Steven protested, clinging to her tightly. This time, it was Minchan who called for a group hug, and they all but mugged her happily.

"We thought you'd never come back!" the youngest whined.

"And miss the chance to do *this*?" Fi reached up to pinch his cheek. "Never."

Minchan's eyes disappeared into uneven crescents as he smiled, and he pulled her close, hugging her tighter.

"Welcome back, Fi." Yihwan reached over to ruffle her hair, a gesture he used to do a lot during their debut days so he could annoy her. He grinned when the telling crease on her brows appeared, and the promise of a fresh, new start made his heart drum loudly against his chest.

Fi raked her hair back in place with her fingers. "Thanks, you guys...I really appreciate this very warm welcome," she said. "But we can celebrate later. We have a 3 o' clock at Jamsil—why aren't you ready yet?"

"Look at you being so tough on us on your first day back," Steven teased.

"Parking lot, five minutes! Last one to get inside the van buys dinner for the entire week. Go!"

All three scampered to pick up their things, mumbling and grumbling about how Fi had changed so quickly. Yihwan was first to head out the door, surprised to see Fi had already left the room.

It was almost noon, but Gabriel didn't feel the need to stand up and grab lunch with everyone else on the floor. Not when he had Singapore on one line and Thailand on another. It was thankfully not a matter of damage control, just opportunities that come a-knockin' at (somewhat) inopportune times.

He saw movement from the partly frosted window of his office and wondered if his sunbae had already gone to the cafeteria with the rest. One of the PR staff members was celebrating his birthday and had promised to treat everyone to a meal. Gabriel wished it wasn't lunch, because he might just get the scraps when he finally showed up.

"Yes, we can arrange for a contract to be drafted between the two agencies, but it's not for me to decide. All I can offer at the moment is—" He paused when he heard something. *Did someone knock?*

"Mr. Park?" he heard the voice on the other line say.

"I'm sorry, uh... hang on, I think the signal's getting choppy." He heard it again—it definitely was a knock, and he got up to see who it was. Probably someone from the team reminding him to get some sort of sustenance.

But the figure he saw was already leaving. When his visitor turned back to look in his direction, his heart raced. There was no way he could be wrong.

"I can offer a recommendation to marketing so they can review your proposal, and I or someone from that department will get back to you as soon as we can." He wondered for a second if Singapore noticed how he was suddenly rushing. And Thailand...Thailand could wait ten more seconds.

Gabriel rushed to open the door. A takeaway bag from the coffee place he likes sat on the carpet, as though it had been deliberately left there for him to see. He picked up the bag and peeked inside, and the soothing aroma of his favorite poison quickly filled his senses. There was even a serving of his favorite grilled chicken sandwich in there.

A note was stapled on the paper bag:

Hey, Mr. Pushover.
See you around. <3
-Chopstick

A grin slowly spread across his face. He probably had more than eight hours left in his work day, but it didn't matter now that he had coffee, his favorite sandwich, *and* his favorite girl out there somewhere, in the same city he's in, waiting to be said hello to.

Gabriel Park, 11:57 am
Hey, thanks for lunch.

Fi Legaspi, 12:00 pm
Figured you'd skip again, you workaholic.

Gabriel Park, 12:02 pm
I learned from the best.

Fi Legaspi, 12:05 pm
Oh no. Are you turning into the old me?

Gabriel Park, 12:06 pm
Depends. What's the old you like?

Fi Legaspi, 12:08 pm
Works too much. Needs to be reminded to breathe a little.

Gabriel Park, 12:09 pm
And the new you?

Fi Legaspi, 12:13 pm
Probably still the same, only less severe.

Gabriel Park, 12:17 pm
Welcome back to AmEnt, Chopstick.

Fi Legaspi, 12:18 pm
Very happy to be back, Mr. Pushover.

Gabriel Park, 12:25 pm
Dinner tonight?

Fi Legaspi, 12:28 pm
If you don't mind the caf, then yes.

Gabriel Park, 12:29 pm
Awesome.

Fi Legaspi, 12:30 pm
♥

THE END.

GABRIEL'S CHECKLIST

(or, how to survive your first Christmas in Manila)

*Gabriel's Checklist appeared in Make My Wish Come True, a
#romanceclass Christmas anthology.
(This happens within the time frame of Scandalized.)*

☐ PACK LIGHT CLOTHING.

4:00 AM, 5 days before Christmas

E ven with nothing but his boxer shorts on, Gabriel Park
tossed and turned in his sleep.

Less than twelve hours ago, he'd flown in with subzero-
degree temperatures in Seoul, and his body was still acclimating to
the humid Manila weather. There was no air conditioning in this
room, but he wasn't going to complain. He was only staying as a
guest here at Filipina Legaspi's house, after all.

He could tell she'd prepared for his short stay, even though
he'd said there was no need to make such a big fuss. The mattress
and pillows were now fitted with new sheets. They came in a rich,
dark blue color, a far cry from the pastel sheets with dainty flower
prints he'd slept on a few months ago.

The room, which belonged to Fi's older sister who worked
overseas, had also been cleared of its clutter. Its walls still proudly
showed off Mayumi's love for old school K-pop, as evidenced by
posters of first-generation idols. On the shelves were K-pop photo
books as well as CDs, organized better than the last time he was
here.

It had been Fi's stories that piqued Gabriel's interest and made
him decide to return to Manila for Christmas. She'd told him
about age-old traditions, delicious delicacies, and fun activities
she'd missed a lot while working in Seoul for years. Her being able

161

to spend Christmas in the Philippines might be more of a circumstance shoved into her hands than anything, but Fi was very happy to be here.

He was too. Now if only he could get some shut-eye.

"Gabe, are you decent?"

Gabriel's eyelids flew open at the sound of Fi's voice. The room was pitch dark, and the only hint of light he could see came from the digital alarm clock sitting on the bedside table. It said 4:00 AM.

He heard a knock on the door. "Gabe?"

Gabriel sat up in bed, rubbing his eyes with the heel of his palms. Why is she up so early?

He replied with a soft groan and got out of bed. Careful not to bump into or trip on anything, he padded cautiously toward the door.

"What is it?" he asked sleepily as soon as he opened the door. The light from down the hall assaulted his eyes, making him squint.

"Jesus Christ, I asked if you were decent!" Fi exclaimed, frowning. She was still wearing her baby blue pajamas and oversized sleep shirt. There was a green bath towel draped over her left shoulder, and a tub of toiletries was nestled against her chest.

"What—I'm not naked," he pointed out, looking down at his boxers as though checking if his statement was true. "Why are you knocking at a man's door at this ungodly hour?"

"Hoy, this is my ate's room, 'no! Eish, jinjja—" Fi stammered, her words an awkward mix of English, Filipino, and Korean. "Put a shirt on, jebal!"

Gabriel laughed, finding it amusing how flustered she was. If he'd felt a little groggy seconds earlier, he was definitely awake now.

"First of all, your sister is not in the room with me." Just to be annoying, he pulled the door wide open and stood at the threshold—one arm leaning against the frame, his free hand resting on his hip. He held back a smile when Fi appeared to be debating in her head whether to take in the view or look away.

"Secondly, I can't sleep in this heat."

She looked up at him, eyes fixed on his face, challenging. "And whose fault is that? I told you to book a hotel so you'd be more comfortable."

"And I told you I want to be with you."

Her lips parted as if to protest, but no words came. Now accustomed to the light down the hall, Gabriel's eyes caught Fi's attempt to conceal a blossoming smile with a pout.

"Just get dressed," she said in a huff and turned to go. "We're hearing mass. Simbang Gabi."

A soft chuckle escaped his throat as he shut the door. All of a sudden, it wasn't such a task to get dressed in the wee hours of the morning. (And on his vacation too.)

Gabriel returned to bed, pulling his suitcase along with him. Several days ago, Fi reminded him to leave the knitted sweaters and goose-down jackets in Seoul because there was no winter in the Philippines. ("Okay, maybe bring just one set, so you don't freeze to death when you fly back.") He ended up revisiting his summer wear and packing his bag with every cotton shirt he could find.

"Okay... what do people wear to mass these days...?" Gabriel mumbled to himself as he unpacked his luggage and organized everything on his bed. Shirts and pants side by side on his left, underwear and socks on his right.

Underneath all the clothes was a flat red box with a gold ribbon tied around it. Gabriel picked it up and smoothed his thumb over the ribbon. It was less than a week until Christmas day, and he couldn't wait to see how Fi would react opening this present.

Will she like it? he wondered. He sincerely hoped she would.

□ ALWAYS BE OPEN TO TRY SOMETHING NEW.

Gabriel was awake for the entire Simbang Gabi.

(Perhaps not for all the right reasons, but he could at least say he didn't doze off in the middle of it.)

While neither of his parents were devout Catholics, Gabriel recalled coming to church and hearing mass as a child. It wasn't frequent, but he also remembered being either so restless or sleepy. He never complained, though. He knew his mother would smack him on the head if he expressed his honest thoughts about mass being boring. Then again, this was the same woman who told him that being a decent person was enough to make God happy.

It was the pomp, he decided, that kept him interested and on his toes today.

The parish near Fi's house was small and unassuming, but the string of lights that outlined its facade created a vision against the dim Manila skyline. Inside, the walls were beautifully adorned with more lights and star-shaped lanterns. From where they were seated, Gabriel could see a nativity scene by the altar, and on the opposite side stood the choir in their white-and-gold robes. Everything looked so festive and put together, it was difficult to feel bored. Good thing too, that the mass was in English.

Fi holding his hand during the Lord's Prayer and kissing him on the cheek as greetings of peace were exchanged jolted him awake as well. The fact that Fi's mother, Diana, was one seat away from him when it happened made him panic for a second, though.

"Would you like some bibingka and puto bumbong?" Diana asked after the mass ended, her gaze flitting between Fi and Gabriel.

Fi answered before he could ask, "They're rice cakes. You should try them."

"Sure." He wasn't very picky with food; he had tried isaw and balut before, after all.

"I'll light the candles, Ma. You go ahead and buy. Pakisabi kay Aling Mercy, damihan naman 'yung niyog..."

Diana only laughed and went ahead of them, and Gabriel watched her get lost in the sea of people (who knew this small structure could fit so many?) leaving the church. Meanwhile, he followed Fi to the back of the church and watched her light prayer candles.

A soft tap on his shoulder made Gabriel turn his head. A familiar face greeted him with a smile.

"Hey, man. When did you arrive?"

164

"Carlos." Out of habit, Gabriel bowed to Fi's friend and smiled. "I flew in yesterday afternoon."

"Awesome. You're spending Christmas and New Year in Manila?"

"Just Christmas. I have a lot of work cut out for me before the year ends."

Carlos clicked his tongue. "Ah, that's too bad."

"Yeah, I would've wanted to spend more time with Fi."

A pleased grin appeared on Carlos' face. "I'm sure she'd love that."

"Really?" Gabriel glanced at Fi who was still standing in front of the wrought-iron candle stand, hands clasped together in prayer. "Doesn't seem like she's too happy about me being here, though."

Carlos laughed and gave him a sympathetic pat on the back. "Filipina's just not used to this kind of attention," he said. "Why don't you try, uh—we have this thing in the Philippines called panliligaw."

"Panli-what?"

"Panliligaw. Courtship," Carlos said. "Ligawan mo si Fi."

Gabriel jerked an eyebrow. Courtship. Huh. In all the years he'd spent in the dating scene, Gabriel never really thought of proper courtship and what it entailed. His past relationships usually followed the "I like you, you like me, let's date" cycle, affairs that ended almost as quickly as they began. His friends in New York, while not conservative in any way, used to lecture him about the difference between serial dating and being an asshole.

You're one hookup away from being a jerk, one of them said. *Watch it.*

Maybe he became that guy, he wasn't sure. All he knew was that he dated more than one girl after that, and then he just sort of walked away from it all, weary of the flirting over drinks, the one-night stands, the "putting your best foot forward" during the first date.

But now Carlos was suggesting he pursue Fi through courtship, and he wasn't really sure he was wired for that.

"Is that... necessary?"

"Well..." Carlos pursed his lips and tilted his head to the side. He appeared to consider Gabriel's words, nodding before he spoke. "It was only a suggestion."

As Gabriel mulled over the idea, Carlos continued speaking. "I know I might have sounded like I'm trying to meddle in your affairs when I shouldn't, but... Filipina is one of my best friends. She's never had a boyfriend before—not because Tita Diana was strict about it, but because she felt like she had to be as good, as smart, and as diligent as her sister. So she studied as hard as Ate Yumi did and barely had time to think about boys and relationships... things like that.

"Knowing you're here because of her makes me happy," Carlos added, the smile on his face sincere. "If there's anyone in the world who deserves to be loved just as much as she loves, it would be Fi. And if I could help in any way..."

Fi appeared beside Carlos all of a sudden, cutting his sentence short. Her arm quickly found a spot over his shoulder. "What are the two of you talking about, hm?" she asked, knocking her head gently against Carlos' before looking up at Gabriel.

Carlos cleared his throat and trained his eyes on Gabriel as well. "Oh, nothing much. I only asked him if he's tried Aling Mercy's puto bumbong yet."

"Oh right! Mama already went to buy some—let's go outside and meet her!" Fi let go of Carlos and led the way out.

Gabriel spoke in a hushed tone as soon as Fi was a safe distance away. "So can you tell me more about this... courtship thing?"

"Is this your way of accepting my suggestion?"

Gabriel caught sight of Fi glancing over her shoulder and beckoning them to move faster. He only nodded at her, then turned to Carlos with a smile.

"You can say I'm always willing to try anything once."

□ BE READY TO PUT YOUR STOMACH TO THE TEST.

8:00 AM

"Diana."

Fi's mother looked up from the tsokolate de batirol she was preparing and cast a gentle smile at Gabriel. "Yes, hijo. Do you need something? Are you hungry? I'm almost done cooking..."

Hungry? Hardly. The rice cakes they ate after coming home from church were filling enough to last him another two hours, at least. But it seemed Diana was in the middle of preparing a meal, if the pans on the stovetop were any indication. There was fried rice in one pan and some sweet-savory sausages in the other. A platter on the kitchen counter had a few fried eggs, cooked sunny-side up.

Is this lunch? But it's only eight o' clock!

Gabriel waved his hand no, a quick response to Diana's question. While the scent of food was heavenly, his stomach twisted in small, painful knots. This only usually happened when he'd done something horribly wrong and had no choice but tell his mother before she found out from someone else. Even the worst of work mishaps weren't enough to make him feel this kind of unease.

"Are you looking for Fi? I think she's napping in her room right now."

"No, I..." Gabriel's words were cut short when Diana left what she was doing on the kitchen counter to mind the sausages in the frying pan. She picked up a pair of tongs and turned each sausage, making sure the side previously submerged in oil was nicely cooked. Fat from the meat made small explosions that made Gabriel flinch, but Diana worked steadily, moving on to the fried rice when she was done with the sausages.

Every movement Diana made in front of the kitchen stove reminded Gabriel of his own mother. For a moment, he wondered what Jean Park was up to in their New York City apartment. Probably snuggled up to her dog—a golden retriever named

Ginger—while watching her favorite show on TV. He smiled at the thought, making a mental note to call her in the morning.

"Let me help you," he offered, scanning the kitchen counter for possible tasks. Chopping, slicing, mixing, maybe? His eyes drifted to the pile of dirty dishes on the sink.

"Naku, hijo. You're a guest here, I can't let you."

"No, please... I insist. I can wash the dishes for you. I'm excellent at washing dishes."

The woman laughed. "You're bored, ano? It's too bad Carlos isn't here—I'm sure you young men can find something to do. Let me wake Fi instead. Sandali—"

Gabriel touched Diana's arm. "Please don't. It's really fine. Actually, I wanted to speak to you too."

"Oh?" Diana looked at him thoughtfully. "What about?"

First of all, you've got to make your intentions known, Carlos had told him earlier. *Not only to Fi, but to her family. It's a form of respect. Not a lot of people do that anymore, but I think Tita Diana will appreciate it. Fi too.*

"I really like Fi," he said, stating the obvious. A smile slowly lifted the corners of Diana's lips as he struggled with his words. "And I, uh—I wanted to let you know that I'm... making lugaw."

The smile on Diana's face broke into a wide grin before laughter took over. "Oh, Gabriel. It's ligaw, not lugaw! Lugaw is porridge!"

"Ah. Right."

"Unless you want to make lugaw for her too, then that's fine."

Gabriel laughed along with Diana, the knots on his stomach finally loosening. "No, I'm pretty sure what you're cooking would be enough. Please let me help you. It's the least I could do for crashing here."

"Oh, shush. You are always welcome here," Diana said. "But if you insist, you can help me with Fi's favorite hot chocolate."

He agreed, and Diana patiently taught him how to whisk melted tablea—pure cacao beans roasted, ground, and molded into small round discs—with a bit of milk and muscovado sugar. She showed him how to work the molinillo, a wooden whisk she held between her palms and rotated as she rubbed her hands together.

"Fi likes it really rich and frothy," Diana offered. "So you have to do a good job whisking the chocolate."

"All right."

"It's a little tricky the first few times, but your hands look strong. I think you'll do well."

And he did, several agonizing minutes later. A proud smile appeared on Gabriel's face when the hot chocolate finally turned nice and frothy under his care. Diana gave him small cups to pour the drink into, and he managed to do so without spilling any of the precious chocolate.

Soon, it seemed that the delicious aroma reached the second floor of the Legaspi household, because Fi shuffled into the dining area just as Gabriel and Diana were setting the table. She didn't seem fully awake yet, but she gravitated toward her usual spot at the table and settled in her seat.

"Oh good, you're awake!" Diana exclaimed. "Let's have breakfast!"

"Good morning, Fi," Gabriel greeted, placing a cup of tsokolate de batirol in front of her.

She looked up at him with a sleepy smile he found terribly endearing. "Good morning, Gabe."

□ PREPARE TO SING WITH ALL YOUR HEART.

Fi tried her best to play hostess for the next three days, taking Gabriel to places he'd never been to the last time he was here. But because she had to factor in Christmas-rush traffic to their travel time, their itinerary was rather limited. He didn't mind.

On the first day, Fi had Carlos (who was already on Christmas break) drive them to Calauan, Laguna, so they could enjoy lunch at a restaurant called Isdaan. Gabriel found the place disorienting at first, what with grand Buddha sculptures displayed alongside cartoon characters and statues of famous people. He enjoyed taking silly photos by the sculptures while waiting for their food to arrive, though.

"Gabe, have you tried eating with your hands?" Carlos asked as platters of fresh seafood cooked in various ways—grilled, baked, sautéed in butter—were placed on their table. Fi giggled.

"No."

"Oh, you really should. The food tastes better that way," Carlos said, leaning over so he could take Gabriel's spoon and fork away. "Fi, do the honors."

Gabriel observed Fi while she picked off a bit of flesh from the grilled tilapia, dipped it in a mixture of soy sauce, calamansi, and crushed pepper, and put it on top of her steamed rice. Then, she gathered the rice and fish into a small ball between her fingers before bringing it into her mouth.

It looked easy enough.

He watched her relish the morsel of food, brushing away a grain of rice by her bottom lip with his thumb.

The gesture made Fi blink twice and look away. She picked up a glass of water and drank from it.

"Fi, are you blushing?" Carlos asked. Gabriel could tell he was fighting the urge to laugh out loud.

Fi shot her friend a glare, then turned to Gabriel. "What are you waiting for?" she snapped. From across the table, Carlos let out a snort, then quickly diverted his attention to his plate.

"Your turn," she told Gabriel.

"Yes, ma'am," he said, unable to suppress a smile upon seeing Fi's cheeks turn a nice shade of pink. Carefully, Gabriel mimicked what Fi had done, but ended up spilling half of the food he picked up with his fingers. It made her laugh, and she spent the next ten minutes teaching him how to eat kamayan style.

He wasn't sure about the logic (or was it some sort of magic?) behind it, but the food did taste better when he used his hands to eat.

Fi took him strolling through Luneta Park the next day, and they enjoyed some dirty ice cream he surprisingly missed. And because he finished a total of five ice cream cones in just a few minutes (in his defense, they were tiny), she began teasing him about it.

"I should look for some ice cream eating contests around... make some good money out of them while you're here."

"This makes me assume you've joined them in the past."

"Not ice cream. Hotdogs."

Gabriel coughed. It took every bit of willpower to keep himself from making a naughty comment, and in the end he just cleared his throat to stifle a laugh.

She threw him a playful punch on the arm. "Don't think I don't know what you're thinking."

"I beg your pardon?" He placed a hand against his chest, as though offended.

With one eyebrow raised, Fi said nothing and just stared at him. He mirrored her expression and stared back, and soon they were laughing like idiots in the middle of the park.

"Come on. Where to next?" Gabriel asked and took her hand. Lifting it slowly to his lips, he watched the tender smile on Fi's face turn into a scowl when he gnawed at her hand instead of kissing it. She shoved her hand to his face and he bolted, laughing, enjoying this—Fi chasing after him for once.

They ran in circles around the park until they both got tired and decided they needed something to drink. "We'll settle this in a more civilized manner later," she said. And he agreed.

A good part of their afternoon was spent getting lost among the paintings and artifacts in the National Museum, which was within walking distance from Luneta Park. Fi brought him to a small turo-turo—literally "to point," because you point at what you want to eat, and they serve it to you. It reminded Gabriel of the hole-in-the-wall Fi liked to frequent back in Seoul: cozy, welcoming, and served tasty meals.

After dinner, she took him for another walk to a nearby wet market where they bought fruits and chestnuts before riding a jeepney back home.

"You're not bored, are you?" she asked him, her voice loud enough to be heard over the Christmas songs blaring from the cramped vehicle's radio.

He shook his head, unsure why she would think that. "Not at all."

On the third day, Gabriel found himself in a karaoke room with Fi and a bunch of her high school friends and their plus-ones. Karaoke was, apparently, as much of a sport in the Philippines as it was in South Korea. Then again, Gabriel had never gone to a karaoke room with friends in Seoul. It was always for a work outing and more about making good with your superiors than having actual fun.

"I'm sorry I had to drag you into this," Fi whispered to him as Carlos belted out a Bon Jovi classic. "I didn't want to leave you alone at home."

He gave her hand a reassuring pat. "It's fine, I'm having fun," he whispered in return. He also kind of fought the urge to kiss her on the cheek, but he let his bottom lip brush against her ear anyway.

There were about fifteen people in the room, twelve of them complete strangers to Gabriel. He wasn't exactly averse to being social, but it was comforting to have Fi sit so close to him. She would often rest her hand on his knee, even. He liked that.

"You do know they're going to make you sing, right?"

"Oh, I know. Don't worry."

She clicked her tongue. "Aigoo. Wipe that confident smirk off your face, aigoo," she said, picking up a piece of chicharon from the selection of snacks on the table and shoving it into Gabriel's mouth.

The piece of deep-fried pork rind made a satisfying crunchy sound between his teeth as he chewed. Carlos had already given him a heads-up about this karaoke session and, more importantly, the possibility of Gabriel getting grilled by their friends.

We're a pretty chill barkada, Carlos had said about their group of friends. *Only two are guys, so we're going to be outnumbered. I'm pretty sure the girls will be charmed even before you say a single word, though. With that face of yours.*

Gabriel couldn't remember why he expected a less-than-friendly atmosphere, but the warm welcome brought him a sense of relief. He did his best to respond to the questions thrown at him, and soon he found himself making small talk about this and that.

"Gabriel—it's your turn to sing!" With the flair of a TV show host, Carlos pointed the microphone toward him. "Do you have a song ready?"

"24552."

Fi's friends cheered when Carlos punched the numbers into the machine and Kiss from a Rose flashed on screen.

"All right, let's see if I'm drunk enough for this!" Gabriel slapped his knees lightly and got up, taking the microphone from Carlos, who urged everyone to clap. The room erupted in cheers. "Good evening, everyone. Sorry for crashing your party."

"Oh shush! Any friend of Fi's is a friend of ours!"

"You mean boyfriend!"

"So is this song for Fi?"

A grin appeared on Gabriel's face. "This. And every song I'm allowed to sing later on."

He wasn't the best singer, but he was a little drunk. Perhaps liquid courage was all he needed so he could make a fool of himself in front of strangers.

Before he came to Seoul years ago, one of Gabriel's side jobs required him to walk down a ramp wearing nothing but underwear. Strangely enough, standing here now made him feel just as naked. Maybe even more.

Was baring his thoughts through song in front of Fi and her friends worse than baring his body? Maybe. But he was already here, so... might as well.

"You actually sing well! And here you said you couldn't sing," were Fi's first words to him when he returned to his seat.

"Never said I couldn't," he corrected, recalling how the Amethyst Entertainment staff tried to persuade Gabriel to sing for the company Christmas party last year. "I said I didn't want to."

"And yet—" She held her arm out toward the small stage area in the room.

Gabriel gave in to his desire to kiss her right then, leaning in to gently press his lips against the side of her face. "This is different," he whispered. "This is for you."

□ LEARN THE LANGUAGE AND USE IT WELL.

8:00 AM, Christmas Eve

"Where's my mom?"

"Hey, good morning," Gabriel said, looking over his shoulder. He saw Fi saunter into the dining area, disheveled hair and all. She took her usual spot at the table and began tying her hair.

"G'morning, Gabe."

"Your mom went to the market to buy something."

"What, you mean the food in this house isn't enough to feed a village?"

He laughed and almost dropped the piece of tapa he was lifting out of the pan with a pair of tongs. "Nae mari," he agreed, neatly putting the portions of cooked meat on two separate plates. He placed a cup of fried rice each on the plates and topped them with a fried egg. Sunny-side up, well done. Just the way Fi liked it.

"Did my mom tell you to take over the kitchen?"

"Hmm, actually—" Gabriel turned around, a plate in each hand. "I volunteered to cook breakfast today."

Fi's eyes lit up all of a sudden. If it was because she just realized he was wearing her mother's pastel-pink apron, or because the food was ready, he wasn't sure.

"Wow. You should wear pink more often."

Ah. Pink apron it is.

"Duly noted, Ms. Legaspi," he said as he put a breakfast plate in front of her. He took in the expression on her face and figured she was a little suspicious about... all this. "Don't worry. I do know how to cook, you know. I've been living alone for years."

She smirked at him. "Did I say anything?"

"No, but you were thinking it." He returned to the counter to pour some freshly made hot chocolate in two cups. He'd liked the process of making tsokolate de batirol so much, he offered to do it for Fi's mom every day since he learned it. Maybe he should buy tablea and bring it with him to Seoul. A sweet reminder of Diana's approval of him pursuing her daughter.

"Fair enough."

"The dishes are easy enough to make, Fi. Did you really think I'm not capable of frying things?" He put her cup of hot chocolate beside her plate, then settled into the chair across from her.

"Fine. Won't we wait for Mom, though?"

"I... lied—she's actually taking a break right now." Gabriel took his apron off and put it aside. "I gave her an early Christmas present."

She shot him a curious look.

"Spa services at a nearby hotel. And buffet breakfast. She'll be back by—" He looked at his watch. "Lunchtime. And she has two friends with her so she wouldn't be lonely."

"Wah. You planned this, didn't you?"

"She'll be fine, Fi. Kain na tayo."

He caught her jerking an eyebrow before the corners of her lips turned up in a smile. Was she impressed at his enunciation? He'd practiced a lot with Carlos' help.

"I see you've been learning Filipino. Is it Carl's idea?"

Gabriel only shrugged and picked up his spoon and fork so he could begin eating. "Jal meogora," he said with a gentle nod.

They ate in silence for a little while and let the noises outside become their music. Silver hitting porcelain mixed with the roaring of tricycles, the shrill yip of the neighbor's dog, and a low voice yelling "Tahoooooo!" made Gabriel smile. In several more hours, he would be hearing someone call out "Balut! Penoy! 'Charon!" as well as children singing Christmas carols, all while playing instruments made of discarded bottle caps and milk cans.

A few more hours after that, and it'll be Christmas day.

He was leaving for Seoul in twenty-four hours, and Gabriel figured this was his last chance to have some alone time with her. The past few days were fun. He'd learned a lot of new things about Fi and life here in Manila, but he needed a quiet moment such as this to tell her things that might otherwise be lost over all the noise. Diana was, thankfully, very generous to let him do what he wanted (so long as he didn't burn the kitchen down).

"Do you want to hear what else Carlos taught me?"

Fi looked up from her plate and narrowed her eyes at him. "Naku! I'm pretty sure he taught you words you can't say in front of my mom."

He stifled in a laugh. She wasn't completely wrong.

"Aside from that."

"Okay." Fi let go of her spoon and fork, took a sip of hot chocolate, and leaned back on her chair. She crossed her arms in front of her chest and said, "Let's hear them, Park haksaeng."

Oh, he'd been Carlos' student, all right, and today was his final examination. Gabriel flashed Fi a wide and ready smile, as though he'd been waiting for this chance his entire life. He set his utensils down as well and pushed his plate forward so he could rest his arms on the table.

"Maganda ka," he began. It wasn't a lie. Even with unruly hair and sleepy eyes, Fi still looked beautiful to him. "Matalino. Malambing. Maalaga."

She propped an elbow on the table and rested her chin in her palm. "Adjectives! I'm impressed!"

"Minsan makyoray."

Fi's eyes grew like saucers and then disappeared as she let out a loud cackle. "Oh. My. God. Did you just—"

Gabriel's feigned confusion. "What?"

He could see how she struggled not to burst out laughing some more, and he knew exactly why. Aside from teaching him some decent Filipino words, Carlos had also given Gabriel an introductory course in gay lingo.

She'll have a good laugh, I'm sure, Carlos had said, laughing as well. *You should totally say it. Who doesn't love a guy who can make them laugh, right?*

She gestured with her hand, encouraging him to continue. "Anything else, Mr. Park?"

"Um... charot?"

Laughter bounced across the walls. Fi's boisterous cackle first, followed by Gabriel's low chuckle. It came to a point where Fi started tearing up, and she had to pause and take another sip of her drink to calm herself down.

Gabriel waited until she was ready to hear more from him again, and when she finally was, he simply said:

"Mahal kita."

She was unable to speak then, eyes fixed on his face for a good, long while. It was as though she was trying to determine if he'd only said the words because he knew them, or because he actually meant them.

He challenged her gaze, knowing she'd heard him loud and clear. If she didn't feel the same way, he would be fine with it. This feeling had simmered quietly in his heart for quite a while, and it was only now that he had the courage to actually say it. There was that kiss a few months ago, sure, but he knew not to consider it as anything but her saying she liked him too. And if he had to wait until she could tell him she loved him as well—then wait, he will.

"Gabe..."

"That wasn't a punch line."

"I know."

Gabriel took a deep breath, then let out a relieved sigh. "I'm not expecting you to say it back, you know. And I know it sounds selfish, but this—telling you that I love you—is more for my sake than yours. I haven't said these words to anyone and meant it as much as I do now. And I know that because now I'm willing to wait until you're ready.

"What's interesting is that Carlos told me the word mahal also means 'expensive.' Dear. Precious. It was only then that I realized it was possible for a single word to perfectly capture everything you are to me, Fi. Mahal kita, and I've never done anything like this before, but... Puwede ba kitang ligawan?"

Light danced in Fi's eyes as they began to brim with tears. She laughed softly, and Gabriel thought he mispronounced the word ligaw again.

"If this is your way of getting me to return to Seoul..."

"You don't have to come back if you don't want to," he quickly said. "I have no other agenda but to tell you that I want to pursue you. This. Us."

"So you'd just hop on a plane so we could go on dates."

"Why not?"

"Just how much does AmEnt pay you?" she asked. Her words were still punctuated with soft laughter, even as tears slid down her cheeks.

"Enough," he simply replied, reaching across the table to wipe her tears away.

"Aigoo, Mr. Park."

Gabriel left his seat then, moving to the empty one beside Fi. He dug into his pocket and pulled out the red gift box he had been keeping in his luggage. "I was going to give this to you tonight, but I figured it'd be busy and all..." he trailed off, putting the box on the table.

Fi gazed at the pretty little box and traced the line the gold ribbon made on the lid. She looked at him. "Shall I open it now?"

"If you wish."

She undid the gold ribbon with a gentle tug, then pulled the lid off. Inside was a heart-shaped charm, gold and dainty, attached to an exquisite gold necklace. Fi admired it for a moment, touching the pendant delicately, as though it'd crumble if she were any less careful.

"It's beautiful," she whispered, smiling up at him.

He took the necklace out of the box and proceeded to put it on her, smiling in satisfaction when he pulled away and saw the tiny heart fall on a spot between her collarbones. "Beautiful," he echoed softly, staring into her eyes now.

"Don't just hop on planes and knock on our door without warning, okay?" she said, the expression on her face shifting to something he was more familiar with—Fi's road manager mode. He liked that. Some days.

"I can't promise you that."

"Gabriel Park."

"This is you saying yes, right?"

"Ask me again," Fi teased.

He let out a laugh, clearing his throat right after. It was difficult to school his expression into one of seriousness, not when his heart was making a happy jig against his rib cage. "Mahal kita, Fi," he said again. "Puwede ba kitang ligawan?"

"I must say... Carlos should consider shifting careers," Fi remarked, grinning. Without another word, she leaned forward and wrapped her arms around his neck. And for every version of her reply—"Oo, puwede. Yes, you can. Ne, hal su isseo."—she pressed a tender kiss on his cheek.

Gabriel held her tight and let her go, only so he could watch her eyes twinkle under his gaze. He had so much more to say, but her face was so close, it was impossible to resist those lips. The words can wait, he decided, leaning in to kiss her chocolate-laced mouth. That was it. He was definitely taking some tablea home.

He took his time, and she let him, her fingers familiarizing themselves with the curve of his jaw as they kissed. She was learning, he realized, sensing how she mimicked the force of his kiss and the rhythm by which he pushed and pulled. He smiled.

"What?" she mumbled.

"You're a fast learner. I like that." Gabriel rewarded her with a gentle nibble on her lower lip, and she responded with another kiss that left both of them breathless.

"We should stop, or I'll get used to these damn kisses and crave them when you're not around." Her hands were still resting on the nape of his neck.

Another kiss. "Tell me so I can book a flight back."

She got even. "Have you ever heard of bankruptcy?"

Two kisses. "I have a feeling you'll still take me in."

"Tsch. You're infuriating, you know that?"

"I've been told."

Fi shook her head and glanced at the table, at their food, almost untouched. "Breakfast, Mr. Park."

Oh, how he'd miss this. Her. Gabriel wished he had more time to spend with Fi, but this was fine. This was perfectly fine. He'll figure everything else out later, but right now he was happy to be given a chance by the woman he loved.

"Maligayang Pasko, Fi."

She smiled and Gabriel saw a fondness in her eyes that wasn't there before. It wasn't the same sparkle he usually saw when she talked to him about her band, or Carlos, or her mother. It was new, and Gabriel wanted to believe it was his.

Fi touched a spot on his cheek and drew an invisible line from there to the base of his jaw. She kissed him again.

"Maligayang Pasko rin sa 'yo, Gabe."

She was the best Christmas gift he'd gotten in years.

THE END.

BONUS CONTENT

548

*548 first appeared in #romanceclass #SayFeels,
a Valentine project by The Reading Belles.
(This happens a few years before Scandalized.)*

"So tell us about a Valentine's Day memory…"

Jo Yihwan realized too late he had let out an audible groan—live on internet broadcast, no less—which was quickly picked up by the female host interviewing them.

"Jo Yihwan-*ssi*… you seem to have remembered something horrible."

"The lack of a Valentine, maybe," Steven Bae interjected. Beside him, the youngest member of East Genesis Project, Song Minchan, stifled a laugh. Yihwan fought the urge to land a smack on the back of Steven's head, but flashed the drummer an incensed grin anyway. *I'll get you later, you pr—*

"Let me rephrase the question then," the host said, laughing softly. Her gaze flitted from Yihwan to Steven to Minchan. "If you *had* a Valentine, which EG Project song would you dedicate to that person?"

Steven chose *Firefly Dreams* from the band's debut album while Minchan went with *Homecoming* from their last one. Yihwan pretended to give the question much thought, but really, he only had one song in mind.

"Mine would probably be *Without Fail*, from our second album," he replied and caught the knowing glances of his band members. Steven, *the bastard*, even went so far as clearing his throat like he was about to divulge a well-kept secret.

Valentine's Day, 4 years ago

"Please tell me you're not planning some cheesy Valentine's Day event."

A knitted gray scarf masked the smile on Yihwan's face as he recalled his girlfriend, Han Haera's apprehensive tone over the phone last night. She had a grand total of four events to attend today, she said, and sneaking out for a date was completely out of the question.

"You underestimate me. Why is that?"

"I don't. I know what you're capable of, and that scares me."

"I'm not careless."

Haera knew that too. Thanks to Yihwan's careful planning (and the reliable heavy-tinted windows of their cars), not a single paparazzi photo of them floated around the internet in these ten months they've been dating. The band leader was confident the news outlets had *nothing* on them, else they'd have been exposed a long time ago. A relationship between a rising actress and an up-and-comer in the music industry was as attractive to paparazzi and entertainment journalists as blood was to sharks after all.

"I'll figure something out."

"Please don't get into trouble."

"You'd still like me if I do."

"We'll see about that."

Clutching a small bouquet of white roses in one hand, Yihwan took a few steps forward when the line in front of him moved. He was still a long way away from the entrance of the jewelry store Haera was having a meet-and-greet event in, but he couldn't really complain. This was *his* idea of a Valentine's Day surprise after all. Besides, his height allowed him a perfect view of her through the shop window, and that was enough for the meantime.

(He had things to say about the unnecessary perm her stylist gave her today, though. It made Haera look older. Was that today's concept?)

"Numbers 320 to 340, please stand by!" a female event organizer who stood by the front door announced, disrupting his train of thought. "Numbers 320 to 340—"

Yihwan glanced at the piece of paper that had his number on it. 548.

"O baek sa ship pal," he mumbled under his breath and wondered how much longer it would take before number 548 could get to the end of the line and meet Han Haera. Maybe another hour? Two? "O sa pal," he murmured repeatedly, grinning when an acrostic poem crossed his mind:

Ojik neoreul
Saranghae
Paleul apeujiman

I only love you, even though my arm hurts read like lyrics Steven would write, but Yihwan borrowed a pen from the lady in front of him and wrote the poem on the piece of paper anyway. As more silly poems crossed his mind, he decided to write something decent for Haera instead as an additional Valentine's Day gift.

"I'm sorry but can I borrow this a little while longer?" he asked the owner of the pen.

"Sure. Oh! You even bought flowers for Haera!" the lady noted, her gaze falling on the bouquet he held. "You must be a big fan."

"Ah." Yihwan's cheeks warmed under the cold February air. If he hadn't pulled his scarf up to his nose, he was certain the lady would've seen him blush. "Yes, I am."

"Me too. She's so pretty. And she can really act, you know? Not like other actresses out there who only look pretty for the camera and don't do much else."

"And she does charity work too, bless her heart," another fan commented, joining the conversation.

Yihwan could only nod, unsure if he should offer his own biased opinions. That Haera could cook a mean budae jjigae wasn't exactly public knowledge, was it? And saying she's an excellent kisser was probably not something he should put out there.

"Gong Yoo would be a perfect match for her."

"Isn't he a little too old, though? Someone a little younger like Kim Soohyun would be better."

As Haera's two female fans jumped from one topic of conversation to another, Yihwan willed himself to focus on the task he'd decided on. He almost got upset when the topic of "suitable leading men" evolved to "suitable boyfriends."

Shutting the noise out, he let the pen bleed words, rhymes that flooded his head every time he raised his eyes and saw Haera's smiling face from the shop window. The words came to him like a bullet train that he had to dig his pockets for something else to write on. But he only had a bunch of receipts, an empty gum wrapper, and...

Bingo.

o   Dorm keys in pocket of your navy blue coat.

o   New pairs of shoes arrived at the dorm. Allocate equally please.

o   Injoo will pick up laundry tomorrow.

A sigh of relief escaped Yihwan when he found their road manager Fi's laundry list of reminders tucked in one of his pockets. Fi often wrote up reminders for each of them and snuck the notes in the pockets of their clothes just in case they forget to check their always-exploding phone inbox.

Thanks, Fi, he thought as he scribbled furiously on the piece of paper. *You're a lifesaver.*

Haera's eyes sparkled in recognition when she locked gazes with #548 who slid his number on the table bottom-side-up.

"Sweet of you to write me a poem," she said, flashing Yihwan a smile he knew was for him and him alone. "Flowers too? Oh, thank you."

"Happy Valentine's Day," he greeted, placing the bouquet on the table. Tucked in between the blooms was a recycled piece of paper carrying the rest of his thoughts. He wondered if she'd mind that the reverse side had another girl's handwriting on it. Maybe not. Haera knew Fi, after all.

"Happy Valentine's Day to you too."

Yihwan noted streaks of black ink on Haera's hands as she signed a poster of herself flaunting an exquisite gold necklace around her delicate neck. It was regrettable that these few seconds could be the only Valentine's Day memory he'd have with her this year, but they will have to do. *There will be other days*, he assured himself. Days he wouldn't have to share her with the rest of the world.

Haera reached for Yihwan's hand as she handed him the signed poster. "You must have been waiting long. Are you cold?"

"I'm all right."

She pulled a hot pack from her coat pocket and pressed it into his palm. The gesture prompted some whispering among the fans in line who have seen it, but Haera didn't seem fazed. Yihwan wasn't, either. He relished the warmth that travelled from the inside of his palm up to his arm, then to his chest, where it settled in and made itself feel at home.

"Stay warm, then."

"You too."

"I'm sure this poem will do its job."

"There's more where that came from."

Her lips turned up in a knowing smirk. "I'd love to read them too."

"Next, please!" an event organizer called out, signalling the end of this Valentine "date." Yihwan squeezed Haera's hand and gave her a bow before being ushered away by one of her managers. He could swear he saw a fleeting "*Hey, do I know you?*" look on the manager's face when their eyes met, but Yihwan kept his head down and said nothing on his way out.

Present day

"I'm not a fan of surprises / or the way you wear your hair / I don't believe in second chances / or that the universe is fair..."

"It's been a while since we performed this song, hasn't it?" Minchan asked, chin perched over Yihwan's shoulder. They were monitoring the broadcast they did hours ago and tried to answer as many fan questions as they could on their channel's message board.

"Yeah."

"But without fail, you / You've turned my world around / Without fail, you've / Made me wish I could drown..."

"Shame," the youngest band member mumbled. "I liked this song a lot."

Yihwan's phone rang, distracting him from the broadcast they were watching. He left the tablet in Minchan's hands and stepped out of their studio to take the call.

"To what do I owe this rare phone call?"

He heard laughter on the other line, and the air around him felt warm all of a sudden. "I chanced upon your broadcast today, is all."

"Sure you're not stalking me, noona?"

"Please. You're not the only celebrity with a dedicated channel, you know."

"Right."

"Anyway, you played *that* song... and I thought to call and say hello."

Yihwan leaned his back against the wall and smiled realizing the sentiment wasn't entirely lost on Haera. "Okay, then. Hello is fine."

'Hello' may be perfect, he thought. For what, he wasn't so sure.

Three minutes and forty-two seconds later, Haera had to go. She told him it was nice to hear his voice again, to hear *that* song again after a long while. She said listening to it made her happy. A tiny part of Yihwan regretted not being able to say he felt the same way too.

Minchan was still monitoring when he returned to the studio. Steven sat there with him, picking out fan questions they should answer.

"So..." Yihwan began, chucking his phone on the couch before plopping down carelessly beside Steven. "What do you think about including *Without Fail* in our next tour's repertoire?"

TARA FREJAS

WITHOUT FAIL
Music and lyrics by Jo Yihwan
(Sophomore Year, 2012)

How do you do it?
How is it possible
That I hear my breath catch
And my lips can't hide a smile
When I'm around you?

You must be magic
And I must be dreaming
Hearing you say "We're a match,"
And "Can you stay with me a while?"
And "Do you like me too?"

I'm not a fan of surprises
Or the way you wear your hair
I don't believe in second chances
Or that the universe is fair

But without fail, you
You've turned my world around
Without fail, you've
Made me wish I could drown

In your eyes, in your arms
In your voice, in your charms
Without fail

Exception to the rule
A one in a million anomaly
The universe was kind to me
After all

Because without fail, you
You've turned my world around
Without fail, you've
Made me wish I could drown

In your laughter, your kiss
In your love, this bliss
Without fail
Without fail

ABOUT THE AUTHOR

TARA FREJAS is a cloud-walker who needs caffeine to fuel her travels. When she's not on work mode, she keeps herself busy by weaving her daydreams into stories.

Aside from her obvious love affair with words and persistent muses, this full-fledged Piscean (who cares what NASA says?) is passionate about being caffeinated, musical theatre, certain genres of music, dance, dogs, good food, and romancing Norae, her ukulele. She owns a male bunny named Max who sometimes tries to nibble on her writing notes.

MORE BOOKS FROM TARA
Paper Planes Back Home | The "Forget You" Brew

Settle the Score/Hustle Play | Waiting in the Wings | Like Nobody's Watching

ANTHOLOGIES | Make My Wish Come True (#romanceclass Christmas anthology) | Summer Crush | Second Wave Summer

GET IN TOUCH WITH TARA
Website: tarafrejas.com
Facebook: fb.com/authortarafrejas
Twitter/Instagram: @tarafrejas
Email: author@tarafrejas.com

THANKS TO

Many thanks to these wonderful people, without whom the first and current imprints of *Scandalized* would not have been possible:

My family (*Daddy*, *Mama*, *Jill*, and *Tita Taba*) and my ClingyGirls (*Kushie*, *Pachi*, *Rix*) for being my constants. Living and dreaming and chasing those dreams would not be as fun without all of you.

Mina V. Esguerra, *Anvil Publishing*, and the *Spark Books* imprint, for putting together and facilitating the #SparkNA workshop that sparked the beginning of this series.

Phim, for being one of the very first people who read my work and encouraged me to keep writing. *Jay* and *Yeyet*, for being my beta readers. *Porcey* for the original illustration and calligraphy + *Chi*, for the photo I used on the cover of the first edition.

Ninang Layla, for being so patient with this manuscript from its first draft, and for loving the AmEnt gang (especially Yihwan, haha). *Ate Gette* and *Liana*, for providing additional input during the book's early stages.

Shaira, for the wonderful art I'm now using on the cover, and hopefully, all the other future *Backstage Pass* covers.

My KPop loves: *TVXQ/Dong Bang Shin Ki* and *FTISLAND*, for being such gorgeous, passionate people who are so good at what you do.

To everyone aboard the #LegaspiPark ship: I love you. ♥

to the #romanceclass community, for being awesome in general…like, all the time. You guys are the best.

#RomanceClass is a community of Filipino authors and readers publishing and reading romance in English.

We are constantly creating new things (books, merch, events) and we'd love to have you on board whether as an author or a reader. Check out our catalogue here:
http://romanceclassbooks.com

Printed in the USA
CPSIA information can be obtained
at www.ICGtesting.com
LVHW071541190923
758675LV00004B/378

9 781520 309019